“You want some water?”

She looked up. Bruce stood beside her, holding out a dented canteen. The sun hit him from behind, surrounding him in a brilliant halo. With the light at his back, his features were shrouded in shadow thrown by his cowboy hat—except his blue eyes, that is.

Her heart skipped a beat. This time, it had nothing to do with the climb. It was all about Bruce.

“Thanks,” she said, reaching for the water. Her hand brushed the back of his hand. Her palm warmed as a current of electricity danced along her skin.

Bruce sucked in a breath.

So, he’d felt it, too.

She took a sip, trying to drown the butterflies that suddenly filled her stomach. Holding up the canteen, she said, “Thanks.”

Taking the bottle, he replaced the top. “Anytime.”

Dear Reader,

Whether *Breaking Point* is your first book in the Texas Law series, or you've been with me from the beginning, welcome! I'm so happy to be writing another book in this world. All these books have been so much fun to write. I love the small town in Texas, along with the cast of characters who has grown with each installment.

One of my favorite things about this book is that Bruce McDaniel was able to have a reprise role. He appears briefly in the second book, *Texas Law: Serial Manhunt*, as the manager of the Double S Ranch. He was such a great person, both kind and reliable, that I knew he needed a romance of his own.

I was happy to introduce him to Hannah Jefferies, a dog trainer, newly arrived in the area. Hannah is a strong and independent woman who is ready to write a new chapter in her life. But after too many heartaches, she doesn't want another romance. What's more, she can sense that Bruce hasn't recovered from the death of his wife several years earlier.

When they find themselves helping a group of Texas Law operatives track an infamous serial killer, Decker Newcombe, through the desert, they have to rely on each other to survive. The chemistry between Bruce and Hannah is undeniable, but will they live long enough for their romance to develop?

I hope you enjoy reading this book as much as I did writing it!

In closing, I'd like to invite you to subscribe to my monthly newsletter. I always share what books, shows and fashions I'm loving, as well as what I'm writing.

You can sign up by going to my website: www.jenbokal.com.

Or using this link: eepurl.com/iCTP3E.

As always,

Jennifer D. Bokal

BREAKING POINT

JENNIFER D. BOKAL

Recycling programs for this product may not exist in your area.

ISBN-13: 978-1-335-47181-9

Breaking Point

For questions and comments about the quality of this book, please contact us at CustomerService@Harlequin.com.

Harlequin Enterprises ULC
22 Adelaide St. West, 41st Floor
Toronto, Ontario M5H 4E3, Canada
www.Harlequin.com

HarperCollins Publishers
Macken House, 39/40 Mayor Street Upper,
Dublin 1, D01 C9W8, Ireland
www.HarperCollins.com

Printed in Lithuania

Jennifer D. Bokal is the author of several books, including the Harlequin Romantic Suspense series Rocky Mountain Justice, Wyoming Nights, Texas Law and several books that are part of the Colton continuity. Happily married to her own alpha male for more than twenty-five years, she enjoys writing stories that explore the wonders of love. Jen and her manly husband have three beautiful grown daughters, two very spoiled dogs and a cat who runs the house.

Books by Jennifer D. Bokal

Harlequin Romantic Suspense

Texas Law

Texas Law: Undercover Justice
Texas Law: Serial Manhunt
Texas Law: Lethal Encounter
Stranded
Desert Pursuit
Breaking Point

The Coltons of Colorado

Colton's Rogue Investigation

The Coltons of New York

Colton's Deadly Affair

The Coltons of Owl Creek

Colton Undercover

The Coltons of Alaska

Colton's Final Showdown

Visit the Author Profile page
at Harlequin.com for more titles.

To John.
I'm glad that I'm spending this lifetime with you!

Prologue

Saturday
11:42 p.m.

Warner Crane was exhausted. After a day of hiking through Texas's Hill Country, he and his friends from college had made camp for the night. It was the second weekend in May, and that meant that it was their annual guys weekend, which had started fourteen years ago following college graduation.

There was Paolo, the comedian of the group. Kent, the party animal. Craig, the charming one. And finally Warner, who was the responsible member. Long ago, it had earned him the unwelcome moniker of Mother Hen. In college, he'd hated the nickname. But as it turned out, being dependable was one of the best ways to win at adulthood.

That was another reason he was so damned tired. Aside from working more than fifty hours a week, he'd left his wife and their six-month old daughter at home. Warner always gave the baby her first feeding at 4:00 a.m. Truly, he would've skipped the trip this year, except his mother-in-law chose this weekend for a visit.

He figured the new grandma wanted time with her daughter and granddaughter.

"I brought a few things for the celebration," said Kent, breaking the silence. They all sat around a firepit, dug into the earth and surrounded by stones. The campsite was on public land. It was remote, without amenities, but still used by groups throughout the year. Light from the flames danced across the angles of Kent's face, giving him a devilish look. He dragged his backpack between his feet and produced a bottle and a baggie of green buds and white rolling papers. "Tequila and the best Purple Haze money can buy."

Warner sat up taller. "Weed? You brought weed? That's not legal in Texas."

"Who cares?" asked Kent. "I bought it at a dispensary down the street from my house—paid sales tax and everything."

"Yeah, your house in Colorado," said Warner, countering his argument.

"Relax, Mother Hen," said Craig. "Besides, after the year I had, I need a drink."

Kent passed the bottle. "Didn't bring any lime or salt. Sorry."

Craig stared at the label. "You got the expensive cush but the cheap booze? What's the matter with you, man?" He twisted the cap, the seal breaking with a crack. Lifting the bottle to his lips, he took a swallow and grimaced. "God, that stuff tastes horrible."

"Yeah," said Paolo. "But after the first two drinks, who cares?"

Warner chuckled. It was true.

"I figured this brand was a throwback to our college days." Kent set his backpack on the ground to serve as a table. He pulled out a paper and poured a seam of buds down the middle. Then he rolled it together, winding the ends tight. Pulling a burning stick from the fire, he touched the red tip to the end of the joint. He inhaled deeply before exhaling a cloud of smoke. The scent of skunk filled the air as he tossed the stick back into the fire. "As is this."

He passed the joint to Craig. He took the weed with a shake of his head. "I'm just sticking with booze tonight. I'm too old to get cross faded."

Warner took the offered joint. He touched the paper to his lips and took in a shallow breath. How was it that he was a grown-assed man and still gave in to peer pressure? He exhaled as a feeling of calm settled over his shoulders. He handed the weed to Paolo. "Here you go."

"So," said Warner, gripping Craig's knee. "How are you doing? Really?"

"Not so good," said Craig, taking another swig from the bottle. He coughed into the back of his hand. "The divorce was rough. Sally got the house. The car. The dog. I got alimony payments and all our shared debt."

Warner knew that a divorce would be expensive. But really, he couldn't imagine life without his wife and their daughter. "Must be rough being alone, too."

He shrugged. "I've been dating a woman from work for the past two months."

"Oh?" Kent took a long inhale of the joint before blowing smoke into the air. "Is it serious?"

Craig took a long drink before answering. “I like her and all, but I don’t see this going anywhere.”

“Why’s that?” asked Warner.

“There’s a bit of an age difference.”

“Like what are we talking?” asked Paolo. “She older or younger?”

Craig lifted the bottle to his lips but didn’t drink. “Younger.”

The joint ended up back in Warner’s hand, although he didn’t recall accepting it. He took a toke. “How much younger?” he asked, the words coming out with a cough.

“A bit,” said Craig.

“Dude. Give us a number,” said Paolo, taking the joint from Warner.

Craig took another drink, wiping his mouth with the back of his hand. “She’s twenty-two. You happy?”

For a moment, there was silence. Then, at once, all three men erupted with laughter. Warner wasn’t sure what was so funny, although tears ran down his cheeks. “Twenty-two.”

“You know that when we started college, she was in kindergarten,” said Paolo. “Is that where you met? Did you go to the campus preschool?”

“Bastards,” Craig mumbled, taking another swig of tequila. “I can’t even drink with you anymore.”

He handed the bottle to Warner. He took a drink. The liquor burned a line to his gut. “Smooth,” he said while trying not to gag.

“What’s smooth?” asked Paolo. “Craig or the cheap tequila?”

Maybe it was mixing marijuana and alcohol. Maybe

it was because his drink of choice was now a double espresso. Or maybe it was because Warner hadn't slept more than six hours in a single stretch for nearly half a year. But whatever the reason, his vision started to waver. His eyelids were heavy. He stared into the fire. The dancing flames were hypnotic.

"Dude." Craig kicked the toe of Warner's boot. "You okay?"

Warner looked at his friend. Craig's silhouette was blurry. "Just tired."

"You should get some sleep now. With kids, you never know when you'll get to rest again." Paolo was the father of four and had been a great resource during these past few months.

Warner stood. The world seemed to tilt beneath his feet.

Kent snorted. "Mother Hen, you are wasted."

Warner flipped them off as he stumbled toward the tent.

He opened the flap and crawled onto his sleeping bag. He was practically asleep before he even closed his eyes.

He didn't know how long he'd been out when the crunch of footfalls by the tent's wall pulled him back to consciousness. Leaning on his elbow, he looked out a mesh window. He could see a man's shadow. He was skinny, with shoulder blades visible beneath his tattered shirt. For a moment, Warner wondered if Kent had spiked the weed and he was hallucinating.

It wasn't until he heard Craig ask, "Dude, who are you?" that he knew the man was real.

"Hey, man. You got some water or something?"

"Sure," said Paolo, reaching into a cooler. He tossed a bottle to the man. "What are you doing all the way out here?"

"Got lost," said the man before he unscrewed the top and took a long drink.

"You got a name?" asked Craig.

The man's voice was like gravel, sharp and loose at the same time. "I'm Decker Newcombe."

All three of Warner's friends began to guffaw. "Good one," said Craig.

The man chuckled, as well.

The laughter died and only the sound of the crackling fire remained.

"I'm not joking," said the man.

Warner had heard of the serial killer. After all, who hadn't? The fact that he was here was unbelievable. Maybe this was all a dream. Yet he scooted farther into the darkness of the tent.

"What do you want?" asked Paolo, a slight tremor in his voice.

"I want your car keys," said Decker.

"Are you high or something?" Kent asked, his words slurred. "I'm not giving you the keys."

That's when the first shot rang out into the night. It was followed by a scream. A yell. Then two more shots interrupted the silence. From the tent, Warner watched it all. The fire from the gun's muzzle. Blood exploding out of wounds as the bullets struck his friends. The limp bodies that slumped on the ground.

The skinny man bent over Kent's corpse, pulling things from the pockets.

Warner's eyes burned and his throat was tight. How could his friends be gone? Still, he couldn't stay put. Certainly, Decker would come to the tent. The killer would find Warner and then he'd be just as dead as his friends.

That left him with only one thing to do.

Run.

Warner pinched the zipper's pull with a finger and his thumb. He tugged slowly as bile rose in the back of his throat. He couldn't get sick now, not when he was trapped in the tent. Inch by inch he lowered the zipper. The teeth unlatched. *ZZZIP.* Warner froze and stared at Decker's back. The killer continued to search through pockets and the cooler. He started again, pulling the zipper free until the tent was open. But Warner was far from safe.

He lifted the tent flap and crawled out into the night. His gaze never left the killer's back as he retreated. One yard. Two. Five. When he was ten yards away, Warner rose to his feet. He took one backward step.

A twig snapped.

Decker stopped moving and looked up. The killer's icy gaze fell on Warner. Without blinking, Decker yanked his gun from the waistband of his pants, aiming the barrel at Warner's chest.

Fire erupted from the muzzle. The bullet flew by Warner's head as he turned, the air sizzling. It struck the ground in front of him, sending a cloud of dirt into the air. Pushing his legs to move, he ran. His feet hit the ground as his lungs burned. His side ached. His head throbbed. He glanced over his shoulder. Decker was behind him, his heaving breaths filling the air with fury.

Another bullet flew past, striking the boulder to his right. Bits of rock exploded, cutting his cheek and neck. Warner ignored the pain and kept running. Three more shots were fired. Then he heard Decker pull the trigger again and again. But nothing happened. Was he out of ammo?

The next time Warner looked back, the killer no longer gave chase.

He could only pray that he'd lost him—but had he?

Feeling as though his lungs would explode, Warner allowed himself to stop, gulping down breaths of air. After a moment, the pounding of his pulse slowed. His lungs loosened. He'd done it. He'd gotten away. But now he had new problems.

He still had no idea where Decker could be.

He was lost in the wilderness with a murderer.

Chapter 1

Monday
6:17 a.m.

The rays of sun broke over the horizon, filling the sky with pinks, blues and oranges. Even though it wasn't officially daybreak, Bruce McDaniel had been at work for nearly forty-five minutes. Then again, as the manager for the Double S Ranch, he always had something he needed to do.

This morning, he sat behind the steering wheel of the two-seater all-terrain vehicle. One of the cows had gotten loose overnight and he wanted to find her before the day got too hot. The trail she left was easy to follow and he steered with one hand. In the other palm, he held the phone to his ear. The engine was loud but driving over the rocky terrain was louder. Still, he could hear enough to carry on a conversation with his daughter, Shana.

"You have to meet the dog trainer who just moved to town," his daughter said. "She's about your age. Plus, she's smart, pretty, and good with animals."

"Are you saying I'm an animal?" he asked, joking.

He'd had this conversation with his daughter more

than once. After seven years as a widower, his adult child was ready for him to start over. The thing was, Bruce wasn't sure how. Maybe it was as easy as letting his daughter fix him up with her new friend. But he hadn't gone out on a date in decades.

Anytime he thought about losing his wife, pain caught in his chest. It was different from those first months after Pamela's death, when the agony was a sharp knife to his heart. Now, it was nothing more than a dull ache.

Swallowing down the grief, he said, "You know that your mother was the perfect woman for me."

Shana let out a long breath, audible even over the growl of the engine. "Mom was wonderful. But she's gone and you aren't. She'd want you to be happy and not to spend your days mourning her."

Bruce ignored his daughter's comment and stopped the utility vehicle. Once he turned off the ignition, the silence enveloped him like a warm blanket on a cold night. After tipping up the brim of his Stetson, he glanced around. The scene was the same as it always was. There were rocks, hills and dirt. All of it held a bright red hue in the morning light. Somehow, he'd lost the cow's trail. He hoped she was nearby.

"You're right," he said. "Your mom wouldn't want me to be unhappy. The thing is, I'm content with my life. My job. You."

"Content and happy aren't the same thing." Why did Shana have to inherit the stubborn gene from him?

Hopping to the ground, he scanned the area again. There was no sign of the missing cow. "I'm old enough to know that sometimes being content is enough."

"Dad, you aren't old."

He'd lost his wife when he was forty-seven. Being a widower at fifty-four years old put Bruce in a difficult place. He wasn't some decrepit geezer, but he also didn't want to start over. Not now, and maybe not ever.

"I really think you should meet my friend. Maybe I can have you both over for dinner one night…"

Shana's words were lost on a primal whine that came from the top of the ridgeline. He peered into the rising sun.

The sound came again. It was an agonized groan. A chill ran up his spine.

Was the cow sick? Injured? Hopefully, neither would be fatal and he'd have enough time to get the heifer to his daughter, who happened to be the local veterinarian.

He started to climb the hill on foot. As he walked, he said, "I didn't say that I'm old, either. But I am old enough to know what I need and want." He paused. Once he crested the hill, there'd be no more cellular signal. "By the way, I might lose coverage in a minute."

"Still haven't found the missing cow?" she asked.

His breath came in short gasps. "I've found something."

The sun shone directly in his face, leaving him blind to everything but the light. Yet he could still see a form lying on the ground. Was it the missing heifer? He couldn't tell. Even if it wasn't, Bruce had a soft spot for all wounded beasts.

He took another step forward and another. As he trudged up the hill, his heart pounded against his ribs with the exertion.

His daughter continued to speak. Saying that her new friend, Hannah, owned a rescue dog.

Or maybe she worked search and rescue with her dog? As much as Bruce loved his daughter, he had quit listening. All his attention was turned to something on the ground. As he got closer, he could see an unruly brown pelt.

No. Pelt wasn't right. What he saw was a head of hair.

The figure on the ground was unmistakably a person. His pulse spiked. Man or woman? From this distance, he couldn't tell.

Bruce sprinted the last five yards. Sliding to his knees, he knelt next to the person. Without question, it was a man. "Hey, buddy." He shook the guy's shoulder. "Can you hear me?"

The guy moaned. Thank God, he was alive. But, what was wrong with him? His lips were cracked. His cheeks were red, and a line of blisters ran across the ridge of his nose. He wore a pair of expensive hiking boots, cargo pants and a long-sleeved shirt. His hands were scraped and raw. The nail on one finger was missing. There were no massive blood stains. No obvious broken bones. Aside from the fact that he was semiconscious and severely sunburned, Bruce couldn't see anything wrong with him.

Then again, he knew that looks could be deceiving. Besides, with a burn like that, he was likely dehydrated.

Bruce pressed the phone to his ear. "Shana," he said, the one word coming out in a rush. "Call 9-1-1. Tell them to meet me at the ranch. I found a man. He's unresponsive."

Nothing.

"Shana?"

After pulling the phone from his ear, Bruce looked at the screen. He had no bars. The call had dropped.

"Dammit." He shoved the device into the front pocket of his jeans.

There was a walkie-talkie in the ATV. But with all the hills, his signal would never reach the receiver back at the ranch. His best plan was to get the guy back to the ATV and call emergency services once he got coverage.

Shaking the man again, he said, "Can you hear me? My name is Bruce McDaniel. I'm going to help you. I'm going to get you down this hill and then we'll get some medical help."

The man's eyelids fluttered. He squinted at Bruce. "They're all dead."

Despite the rising sun, gooseflesh rose on his arms. "Dead?"

The man touched one of the pockets on his pants. "He came out of nowhere and demanded keys to the car. Then he shot them all. I didn't have time to think or even help. But I have the keys, and because of me, they're all gone."

Bruce was afraid he knew the answer, yet he asked the question anyway. "Who was the shooter?"

The man's gaze focused, his eyes meeting Bruce's. "It was that killer. Decker Newcombe."

For a moment, Bruce's face was cold. His hands were numb. His chest squeezed, making it hard to draw a breath. The most dangerous—and notorious—serial killer in decades was on the run in Hill Country.

Narrowing his eyes, he scanned the hillside, looking

for Decker—or a clue as to where he might've gone. There were no broken branches. No footprints in the soil. No trail of blood to follow.

Like all the times before, Bruce knew that the killer had escaped without a trace.

Regardless, they were too exposed on the ridgeline.

"I got an ATV at the bottom of the hill." Bruce slipped his shoulder under the man's arm. "We gotta get you to your feet." Using all the muscles in his thighs, he pulled the guy onto his feet. The man groaned.

Damn. "What's wrong? Is something hurt?"

"All of them," he said, the words coming out as a sob. "He killed them all."

Something was wrong. The man was clearly delusional, given his dehydration. He just didn't seem injured in the physical sense.

Still, if he was going to save the man's life, he had to get him to the ATV and then to the ranch. Supporting most of the guy's weight, he started down the hill. The man's feet dragged in the dirt. Bruce considered picking the guy up and carrying him, fireman-style. But he wasn't sure that his knees could take the extra weight. Instead, he continued, dragging the man as he shuffle-stepped down the hill. "Tell me your name."

"Warner." The single word came out as a whisper.

"Where are you from, Warner?"

"Wimberley," he said.

Bruce was familiar with the small town, even though he'd never been there himself. He continued, trying to keep Warner from Wimberley focused. "You got someone who's missing you?"

"My wife," he said. "Thank God that she and the baby were nowhere near when this happened."

"Let's get you off this hill and you can reach out once we get a phone signal."

The promise of a call to his family seemed to give Warner a strength he didn't have before. The man straightened a touch, taking some of the load off Bruce. They moved quicker.

At the ATV, Bruce guided Warner to the passenger seat. "You wait here," he said, as if the man was going to go anywhere. "I got a cooler with bottled water in the bed." He rounded to the back of the vehicle and lifted the lid. From inside the cooler, he removed three plastic bottles. Two were for Warner. One was for himself. With all the bottles tucked into the crook of his elbow, he removed his cell phone from his pocket. There were three missed calls from Shana. As much as he wanted to speak to his daughter, calling her back would need to wait.

Warner was slumped in the seat, his chin resting on his chest. He opened his eyes as Bruce approached.

"I got you this." Bruce held out one of the bottles. He placed the other two into cupholders attached to the dashboard. Sliding behind the steering wheel, he turned the key to start the ignition. "Take it easy with the water at first. I don't want you to get sick from drinking fast on an empty stomach."

Warner twisted off the cap. He put the bottle to his lips and took a sip. He exhaled. "I don't know how much longer I would've made it if you hadn't come along."

Living on a ranch, Bruce had come face-to-face with death more than once. By his estimation, the man wouldn't have survived another day. He didn't give voice to his thoughts. There was no need. Putting the gearshift into Drive, he pressed his foot onto the accelerator and turned in a wide circle.

He glanced at his passenger. "What happened out there?"

Warner took a sip of water and shook his head. "It was awful."

"Where were you? What were you doing? When did you last see Decker?" Bruce knew that he'd rapid-fired questions at the man, who was not in a good place emotionally or physically. He paused a moment before adding, "The police will need to know."

"It's a guy's trip," Warner said, his voice hoarse. "We do it every year. Did it, I suppose." He wiped an eye with his shoulder. "We carried in our gear and set up camp near Ghost Horse Point." Bruce knew the rock formation. It was about five miles from a state-maintained parking lot. "It was dark. We were sitting around the campfire. One of the guys had brought tequila and pot. I don't drink often and never smoke, and I guess that's what saved my life." He shook his head and took another swig of water. "I went to the tent to sleep. Decker's arrival woke me up. He shot them all—and I ran."

"When did this happen?"

"Saturday night." Warner lifted the bottle to his lips but didn't drink. "What day is it now?"

"Monday morning," said Bruce. "You finish all that water—but slowly. I'm going to make a call." After pulling the cell from his pocket, he opened the phone app and called 9-1-1.

The phone rang three times before being answered by a male operator.

"This is Bruce McDaniel," he said, raising his voice to be heard over the engine noise. "I was out looking for a missing cow this morning when I found a man who got lost. I'm bringing him back to the Double S Ranch. Send an ambulance to meet me."

"What can you tell me about the patient?" asked the operator. "Is he injured?"

It was the same thing Bruce had wondered himself. "He's dehydrated, and has severe sunburn," he said, glancing at Warner. The other man had taken several sips of water. But so far he hadn't guzzled the whole bottle. It was a good sign that he'd be able to keep the water down and recover quickly. "I can't tell if there's anything else wrong with him physically. But..."

"But what?" the dispatcher coaxed.

"But he says that Decker Newcombe raided his campsite and killed all his friends. He also says that he barely escaped." Until now, Bruce hadn't questioned Warner's story. But what if everything was a lie? If Warner had murdered his friends, it would be convenient to blame the homicide on the notorious serial killer. But why get lost and almost die himself?

No. Warner was telling the truth. And if not? Well, answering that question was up to the police. All he could do was get the man the help he needed.

That's when he realized that several seconds had passed in silence. Had the call dropped?

Pulling the phone from his ear, he glanced at the

screen. He still had two bars. The seconds of the call still ticked by. He put the cell next to his ear again. "Hello?"

"Yeah," said the man. "Hello. I'm here. Did you say that the man…"

"Warner. He's from Wimberly."

"He says he saw Decker Newcombe?"

"He attacked their camp near Ghost Horse Point on Saturday night."

The dispatcher said, "An ambulance is on the way. I'm sending a sheriff's deputy to meet you, too."

"I'll be there in fifteen minutes," he said to the dispatcher.

He ended the call with the press of his thumb. Bruce really should call Shana back. There was no telling what she'd heard, and he hated for her to worry. Then again, he'd also promised the phone to Warner. He held out the cell. "Here you go," he said. "Call your wife. Tell her I'm taking you to the Double S Ranch. It's outside of Mercy."

Warner had finished one bottle of water. "Thanks."

Warner took the phone and entered a set of numbers before hitting the call icon. As the phone rang, he reached for one of the remaining water bottles. He unscrewed the cap and took a drink as a woman answered. "Hello?"

Bruce did his damnedest not to listen to the other man's conversation. It was easier than he imagined since his mind was occupied with what needed to happen next. He had to warn his boss, Sage Sauer, and her live-in partner, Michael O'Brien. After all, Decker had come to the Double S to try to kill Michael. True, it had been months earlier. But they still needed to know.

He never did get the chance to make the call. Warner kept the phone pressed to his ear, talking to his wife and sharing details of the horrible experience. By the time he'd said all he'd needed to say, the fencing surrounding the upper pasture for the Double S was visible.

"Here you go," said Warner, holding out the phone.

"Toss it in there," he said, nodding toward the empty cupholder.

Bruce scanned the horizon, searching for the red strobing lights of an approaching ambulance. There was nothing. He could see the house, a white ramshackle dwelling that had been built over generations, and a red barn nearby. Sage's pickup truck was gone. But Michael's blue EV was still plugged into the charger.

He parked next to the EV at the same moment the front door opened. Michael came out of the house, dressed in a pair of khakis, leather sneakers and a button-up shirt. It didn't matter that he lived on a ranch outside Mercy, Texas, now. Bruce imagined that Michael would always look exactly like what he was—a physician from San Antonio.

Waving as he put the ATV into Park, he called out, "A little help here."

Michael's gaze rested on Warner for an instant before he sprinted down the steps. He called out, "What happened?"

"Found him when I went looking for a missing cow. He's been lost for a few days." He paused before adding, "I called Dispatch. They're sending an ambulance. But there's something you need to know. He says that Decker Newcombe killed his friends."

"We'll talk about that later," he said, placing a hand on Warner's arm. "My name's Michael O'Brien. I'm a doctor."

That bit was true. He had attended medical school, but was a forensic pathologist by trade. The way Bruce figured it, right now, any doctor was good enough.

Michael continued. "Can you tell me your name?"

"Warner." His voice was stronger than when Bruce had found him. It was a good sign.

In the distance there was a siren's wail. An instant later, Bruce could see lights on the county route that ran parallel to the property.

Michael asked, "When was the last time you had anything to eat or drink? Are you injured?"

Warner held up a bottle that was half full. "I've already finished this and one other water." He paused. "Before that, it was Saturday evening."

"It's good that everything appears to be staying down."

For the next several minutes, Michael treated Warner. He was moved into the shade and a cool cloth was placed on the back of his neck. His shoes and socks were removed. Bruce was glad to see that the correct care was being given. Yet, all he could think about was the fact that the killer was still out there.

An ambulance turned onto the long drive that led to the house. Michael looked over his shoulder before turning back to Warner. "I'm going to let the paramedics assess you. They have everything they need to make sure that you're stable. Then, they'll take you to the hospital."

Warner nodded as the ambulance stopped next to

the ATV. A cloud of dust billowed up from the tires. It hung in the still morning air before settling back on the ground. A pair of paramedics in blue uniforms jumped down from the ambulance and approached.

Bruce stepped back. He knew when he was needed. He also knew when he was not. Right now, he'd just get in the way.

One of the paramedics held a stethoscope to Warner's chest. The other prepped his arm so they could hook up a bag of saline that was attached to a telescoping pole.

Michael walked to where Bruce was standing. "Good thing you found that guy. With this heat, he wouldn't have lasted the day."

Bruce sniffed, acknowledging the praise. But there was more to discuss than finding the lost hiker. "He said that his friends were attacked and killed by Decker Newcombe. Said that he barely got away."

Michael sucked in a quick breath. "Do you think he's telling the truth?"

Honestly, Bruce believed every word that Warner said. "I think that if we search the area around Ghost Point, we're going to find bodies. It's a possibility that Decker killed those men. But I know for certain that we have to check it out. Who knows what could have been going on out there? We should try to get his full story first."

"You said *we*. Does that mean you're willing to help? Nobody knows this country better than you, Bruce."

He hadn't intended to become a part of the investigation. But why not? He could assign a few of the other ranch hands to find the missing cow. "Let me think about it."

"Think quick," said Michael. Bruce knew what was on the doctor's mind. Decker had followed Michael to the ranch and tried to kill both him and Sage. He imagined that Michael still had scars from the stab wound the killer had delivered. But like with Warner, not all injuries were physical. "I need to make some calls. We have to get a search party to find Decker before his trail goes cold again."

Two things happened at once. The ambulance, with Warner inside, drove away, and Michael stepped back from where Bruce stood to place a call.

Folding his arms across his chest, he looked out at the hills surrounding the ranch. The red soil glowed with the rays of the rising sun. A scraggy tree stood near a split rail fence. This country was more than his workplace and home. The earth was knit into his bones. He'd spent days in the hills while looking for lost cattle or driving the herd northward to market. He knew this country as well as he knew himself—maybe he knew it better. For far too long, Decker Newcombe had turned this place into a killing ground. It was high time that someone stopped the murderer, and he knew he was just the man to lead the team right to him.

Chapter 2

Though it was barely past sunrise, Hannah Jefferies had started her Monday with an early appointment. She wore a blue tank top and faded jeans. At her neck was a silver chain—the only jewelry she wore. Her hair—mostly dark with more than a few strands of gray—was pulled into a low ponytail.

Holding up a single finger, she gave the command. "Sit."

Her newest client, a mixed-breed hound named Old Blue, dropped his rump onto the ground. After pulling a treat from her pocket, she held her hand out in front of the dog. The pooch gobbled the kibble from her palm. She scratched behind one of his floppy ears. "Good boy."

Next, she pointed to the ground. "Lay down."

Old Blue looked at her and yawned.

"Lay down." This time she dropped her voice by an octave.

The dog lay on his stomach and rested his head on his paws. She gave him another treat before petting the top of his head. She turned to Old Blue's person, Ryan Steele. For the most part, Hannah worked with her canine clients and their humans only between 9:00 a.m.

and 5:00 p.m. But for Ryan, she'd made an exception. She was new to the community and needed to build a customer base for her dog training business. When he'd asked for an early appointment, she was simply happy to have a client and ready to accommodate.

"So," she said, not willing to make any recommendations yet. "Tell me about Old Blue. How long have you had him?"

"He's been my pal for a few years," he said. Rising from the ground, the dog came to Ryan and sat next to his feet.

If Hannah had to guess, she'd say that Old Blue was every bit of nine years old. "What do you know about his life before?"

Ryan wore jeans, dusty cowboy boots and a flannel shirt. His dark hair skimmed the top of his collar. He rubbed the dog's neck. Blue closed his eyes and leaned into his person. "I don't know much about his life before he came to me, but he belonged to an elderly couple who died."

Obviously, the dog trusted and loved Ryan. But he could be reacting to something from his past. She gave a sympathetic tut for the former owners. "Did they die of old age?"

Ryan shook his head. "Not old age." He paused an instant before saying, "They were murdered."

Hannah sucked in a sharp breath. "Murdered. What exactly happened?"

Another pause. "I assume you've heard of Decker Newcombe."

Of course she'd heard of the serial killer who had

murdered several people in her new home base of Mercy, Texas, and the nearby community of Encantador. He'd escaped a couple of weeks ago while being transported to jail from the hospital in San Antonio. Now, the killer was at large and considered armed and extremely dangerous.

Did she like the idea of living in the same geographic area where a serial killer hunted? Absolutely not. But the fact that Mercy and Encantador had become tarnished by Decker Newcombe was what made it an affordable place to live and work. After years of paying Dallas metro prices, she was thrilled at the cost for two acres of land, which included a house and enough space for her training facility and, eventually, a kennel.

Hannah exhaled a long, slow breath. "Decker Newcombe," she echoed. "So, this dog's owners were two of his victims?"

Ryan gave a single nod. "Decker set their house on fire. It would've been easy to leave Old Blue. But he didn't. He took him when he left."

Resting her hand on the dog's head, she couldn't help but wonder what the animal had witnessed. No wonder he was acting out. "I guess Mr. Newcombe isn't all bad."

"Trust me," he said with a snort. "He's as bad as they come. But he did the right thing by Old Blue."

The dog licked the air, sensing a change in Ryan's tone. The owner absently scratched behind the canine's ear. To Hannah, it looked like the two understood and cared deeply for each other. She was always happy when dog and person were so well bonded.

While stroking his dog's ear, Ryan continued. "That

night, Decker escaped. It's too bad that you weren't around back then. We could've used someone with the experience to track a person through a storm." He paused. "I checked out your website."

In Dallas, she'd worked with law enforcement on several manhunts. She'd mentioned the fact in her bio on the "About Us" page. Never someone as notorious as Decker Newcombe, though. Still… "If I'd lived here at the time, I would've been out there with you."

For a moment, he silently ran his fingers over the dog's nape. Old Blue gave a contented sigh.

She couldn't guess what Ryan was thinking or reliving in his mind. But his story brought up another mystery. "How'd you two end up together?"

"Me and the dog?" he asked. "I was part of the group who tried to arrest Decker at Christmastime a while back. He had the dog with him, but when he escaped, he left the dog. I'd been shot and while I waited for the ambulance, Blue sat next to me. I guess in the trauma, we got attached to each other." He exhaled. "Once I got out of the hospital, I went to the shelter and adopted him. He's been my best friend ever since."

"A good outcome of a horrible situation," she said.

"For a while, it was just me and Old Blue," he said, stroking the dog's spine. "A few months back, I moved in with my girlfriend. She has two teenaged children. At first, Blue liked having a family. But Kathryn and I decided to make it official and we're getting married at the end of this month." He paused and rubbed the back of his own neck. "To be honest, Old Blue started chewing on the furniture when wedding planning started. I don't know if there's a connection..." Sighing, he shook his head.

At fifty years old, Hannah had been married and divorced twice. While she hadn't exactly left Dallas to avoid her second husband, she was happy to put plenty of miles between her and his constant requests for money. It seemed like she was destined to fall for a guy hard, only to learn his true nature once it was too late. Right now, she was content to stay single and independent.

Ryan's mention of a fiancée was a bit of a surprise, but Hannah didn't begrudge anyone else's happily-ever-after. She'd just given up on the idea of such things for herself.

"Usually, destructive chewing in older dogs is a way to express anxiety," she said, returning her attention to Ryan and his visit. "My guess is that Old Blue is reacting to all the changes and excitement of the wedding planning. Plus, Blue might miss having you all to himself."

After thinking for a moment, Ryan asked "What do I do about it?"

He'd already taken the dog to the local vet, Shana McDaniel. Since there'd been nothing physically wrong with the dog, she'd recommended a training session with Hannah.

"Give him plenty of things he can chew. Take him on a daily walk. Play fetch in the yard. We can also keep working on commands." Hannah paused. "Have you thought about including your dog in the wedding?"

"You know," he said, drawing out the words. "I saw something that might be cute, but I wasn't sure if Old

Blue could handle it." He spent a few minutes going over his thoughts.

"I totally think that's doable," she said. "I'd be happy to set up some sessions so we can work together."

"You'd have to come to the wedding," he said before adding, "Not as the trainer. But if we can pull this off, you'll have to see it for yourself. I'll send you the link for the wedding website."

"Thanks," she said. Hannah was eager to meet new people—not just prospective clients, either. If she was going to live in Mercy, then she wanted to make friends. "That would be nice."

Before Ryan could say anything else, he drew his brows together. Holding up a finger, he pulled a cell from the front pocket of his jeans. The screen glowed with an incoming call. Hannah figured that the device had been set to vibrate. He swiped the call open and held the phone to his ear.

"Hello?" He paused. "Hello?"

Glancing at the phone, he cursed. "Dropped call. It's my boss and, with everything going on, I'd hate to miss something important."

The spotty cellular coverage was one thing that Hannah didn't like about her new home. In Dallas, her phone always had bars. Here? Well, it was anyone's guess what kind of connection they'd get.

"The service is better close to the house," she said, walking toward her home. Ryan and Old Blue followed, trailing her like a boat's wake. "You can come inside, if you'd like."

The training setup was surrounded with a high chain-link fence. The yard was filled with all the equipment she used for agility training. There were hurdles of various heights. Two slalom courses. A PVC tunnel alongside a series of hoops.

Old Blue sniffed one of the hoops as he passed.

"Looks like that old dog is interested in learning some new tricks," Hannah said, turning the adage sideways.

"Do a lot of folks come to you for agility training?" Ryan asked.

"So far, I don't have a ton of clients," said Hannah. Then she suggested, "This might be the perfect place for you and Old Blue to spend time together." She opened a gate in the fence, holding it as Ryan and his canine companion stepped through.

"I'd like to set up an appointment to come back," said Ryan. "We can work on my idea for the wedding, and maybe some agility training after the ceremony."

Her home, an old farmhouse with two stories and a wraparound porch, sat twenty yards from the fenced-in area. Sure, the place needed some work—new paint on the trim and a section of the porch railing had to be replaced. But it was roomier than her condo in Dallas—and what's more, all the property belonged to Hannah.

"You can come inside. I'll grab my calendar and we can set up a time to meet again." She opened back the door. It led to her kitchen. The last owners had updated everything—countertops, cabinets, flooring and appliances. The room gleamed with stainless steel and white. A wooden table for four that she'd brought with the move stood in the middle of the room. A single packing container, the last one to be unpacked, sat in the corner.

"Make yourself comfortable," she said as Ryan walked through the open doorway. "The coffee in the pot is fresh. I grind my own beans, so it's pretty good. Help yourself to a cup if you'd like. I'll give you some privacy to make your call and be right back."

Hannah pushed through a swinging door and left Ryan, along with Old Blue, to contact his boss. She walked down the hall and entered her office. Her dog, a Labrador mix named Gypsum, lay on a rug next to her desk. She looked up as Hannah entered, her tail beating on the floor like it was a bass drum.

"Hey, girl." She rubbed the dog's head.

On the corner of her desk, plugged into an outlet, was her tablet computer. She opened the calendar app. Even though she had a link to sign up for appointments on her website, most slots were open. Hannah had moved to Mercy at the beginning of April. After six weeks in the area, she wanted to be more established. The money from selling her condo and business was running out. Something needed to change, and soon. With an exhale, she tucked the computer under her arm. "It'll just take time."

She decided to look on the bright side of not having any clients. She'd been plagued by hot flashes and insomnia all night. It was all part of being perimenopausal, though it didn't make having sweaty sheets and sleepless nights any better. But an open schedule meant she'd have time for an afternoon nap.

"You wait here," she said, glancing at her dog. Gypsum gave a happy bark. "I'll be right back."

With the computer in hand, Hannah walked back to

the kitchen. Placing her hand on the door, she started to push it open. Then, she heard Ryan's voice and stopped.

"Are you kidding?" he asked. "He's been spotted again?"

Hannah could hear another male voice clearly—almost like the guy was in the room. She assumed that Ryan had turned on his phone's speaker function. "Decker attacked a group of campers. There was only one survivor."

The words sent a chill down her spine. He could only be referring to the infamous serial killer, Decker Newcombe.

So, he was still at large. Hannah shuddered. That couldn't be good for anyone living in the area. They would all be locking their doors for the time being... not that a lock had ever stopped Decker.

"We need to get a group of people to check out the area," Ryan went on. "I'll send all the new hires, along with a tracker. I've been trying to find someone with a search dog who is close and also has an open schedule. The feds and the state police took out K-9 units when the chopper first went down. But the dogs didn't turn up anything. Now, we know where he's been. It might be different."

A moment of silence followed. Ryan then said, "I have just the person. The trainer I brought Old Blue to see has experience with search and rescue. I'm at her place now and can check her availability."

Hannah knew that Ryan meant her. But was she willing to go into the desert to find someone as dangerous as Decker Newcombe? Sure, she'd helped the police search for a number of fugitives. None of them happy to be found. But it was also true that none was as infamous as the man they were looking for now.

In fact, she knew one of Decker's victims—or knew of him in a roundabout way. Decker had beaten a man half to death before Christmas a few years back. Phil had run a restaurant in downtown Encantador. This place, the one she'd bought, had been his home. The injuries sustained in the attack had prevented him from living alone; he'd had to move in with his son and daughter-in-law.

In a way, she felt like she owed it to the former owner to accept this assignment. She would be able to give him the justice that he deserved.

But there was also another truth—and one she couldn't ignore.

Hannah needed the work. Getting established in Mercy had been slow. If she wanted to earn a living wage, she couldn't be too particular about which clients she took on. Inhaling deeply, she emptied her lungs in a single gust. Then she pushed the door open and entered the kitchen.

Ryan stood by the table. He glimpsed her as she entered. To the man on the phone, he said, "Let me call you back." With the press of a button, he ended the call. "I was just talking to my boss, Isaac."

She nodded, not sure what to say. Did she admit to eavesdropping? Or did she let him go through his pitch, even though she'd already made up her mind? In the end, she decided that the best path was usually the shortest.

"I know," she said. "I heard. Decker's been spotted and you want me to help you to find him."

"It's not just me you'd be helping," he said. "You'd be helping the whole community. Besides," he added, "think of the publicity you'll get once he's captured."

Okay, that was an aspect she hadn't considered. Helping to find someone like Decker would definitely be a big selling point for her services. She paused a beat. "I saw a documentary about Decker. It said that he's a descendant of Jack the Ripper—you know, the serial killer from London. Victorian era, I think. Is that true?"

"Yeah," said Ryan. "There was some clothing from one of the Ripper's victims that was still around. As you can imagine, the fabric was bloody. Technology finally got good enough to pull DNA off the cloth. There were only two separate types of blood found—that of the victim and her assumed killer. The Ripper's information was entered into a database to see if any descendants had a criminal history and boom. There was a hit with Decker."

According to the documentary, Decker had started killing women in the same way as his murderous ancestor. "What does he want? Why does he kill?"

"Sometimes, it's for money. But I really think he likes control. The power. The pain." He paused. "I honestly think he wants to become a legend. Just like Jack the Ripper."

Hannah shuddered. "So he really is as dangerous as they say."

Ryan gave a long exhale as he eyed Old Blue. His silence said more than his words ever would. "Come to my office for the briefing this morning at seven thirty. If you don't think our plan is solid, you can walk away. No hard feelings."

Hannah's throat had gone dry. Her palms were sweaty. But this was a once in a lifetime opportunity. If she didn't act now, she'd never get the chance again. Yet she knew something else. All the fame in the world would do her no good if she ended up dead.

Hannah arrived at the Mercy satellite office of Texas Law. Her trained search dog, Gypsum, sat on the passenger seat of her SUV. The offices were located in a renovated one-story motor inn. A dozen doors stood in a line and faced a large parking lot.

Several of the parking spaces were filled. After pulling into an empty spot, she shifted in Park. "Well," she said, the word coming out as a sigh. Whatever misgivings had plagued her earlier were now gone. She had packed a backpack with all the gear she'd need for several days in the desert. It sat on the floorboard behind her seat. "Are you ready for this?"

Gypsum started to pant. Hannah clipped a leash to the harness that was secured around the canine's chest. After opening the driver's-side door, she hopped to the ground. A bead of sweat rolled from the nape of her neck before being absorbed into the collar of her shirt.

"C'mon, girl," she called out with a slap to her leg.

Gypsum climbed over the console between the seats and sprang from the truck. While they crossed the parking lot, Hannah reminded herself of one important thing. She and her dog had been a part of dozens of searches.

Sure, she was new to the community. And true, the missing person was a serial murderer. But none of that changed the fact that she and her dog knew what to do.

Pausing on the sidewalk, she scanned the building. Next to the doors, blue plastic signs had been affixed to cinder block walls: Texas Rangers. Encantador Sheriff. Workout Room. There were three doors for Texas Law—the agency where Ryan Steele had told her he worked. The middle door was marked "Public Entrance."

Stepping up to the door, she twisted the knob and pushed the door open. She entered the room. It was an office, furnished with two desks and a sofa. There was a minifridge shoved into the corner. Then again, the furnishings were difficult to see—the room was also filled with bodies. Eight people, by her count. Aside from one other woman who wore the dark uniform of a sheriff's deputy, Hannah was the only female. With so many people gathered in one small room, the air was thick with body heat and the buzz of hushed conversations.

Ryan nodded a greeting as she stepped inside. Hannah gave a small nod before moving to the corner with the minifridge. Gypsum sat, leaning against her leg.

Striding into the center of the room, Ryan raised his hands. The talking stopped.

"I want to thank everyone for coming on such short notice. As you know, this is a time-sensitive investigation. We have a very credible sighting of Decker Newcombe near Ghost Horse Point. The witness claims that Newcombe killed three of his companions and was looking for keys to a vehicle." He paused. "It'd make sense that Decker is looking for a car of some kind. After all, he lost all his help. The hacker who had been supporting Decker for the past few months, helping to get him cash and information on his victims, was finally arrested a few weeks ago. So basically, Decker is flying solo."

"I have questions about this witness." A man raised his hand. He was young, fit, and reminded Hannah of a puppy who had yet to be housebroken. On either side of him were similarly young, fit men. "What are the chances that this witness did something to his friends and is blaming it on Decker?"

Another man, who looked older than the rest—maybe early to mid-fifties—stepped away from the corner on the opposite side of the room. He wore a cowboy hat and pushed the brim up as he spoke. "I thought he might be lying, too. Blaming Decker would be an easy way to get off scot-free. But when I found him, he was really dehydrated and upset about his friends. If he was the one who killed everyone—I'd be surprised." He took a step back, lowering the hat once more.

"And who are you?" one of the younger men asked.

"Bruce McDaniel," said the older man. Even with the brim pulled low, she could tell that his eyes were a brilliant shade of aqua blue. He glanced in her direction and her heart skipped a beat. "I found the witness."

"So you said. But what is it that you do?"

"I manage the Double S Ranch," said Bruce.

"Bruce knows this area better than anyone else," said Ryan. "He's also going to be the one who'll be your guide. You've all been handpicked for this search." Ryan pointed to a young man with a black crew cut. "This is

Trey. He's newly hired with Texas Law. Just got out of the army."

"I was with the hundred and first. Airborne," Trey offered. "I'll be going out to find Decker and bring him back—with Bruce's help, of course."

The man on Trey's left, with wavy blond hair, was Slade—last name, not first. He was also former military, recently hired by Texas Law, and would be part of the search party as a communications expert. Next, Ryan introduced Ezra—another new hire—who was a crime scene tech. Formerly from the Miami Police Department, Ezra was compact with broad shoulders and dark hair and eyes.

There were other people who wouldn't be a part of the search party per se. The woman, she learned, was the local undersheriff from Encantador, Kathryn Glass. She wore a tan uniform, and her dark hair was pulled into a ponytail. There was a helicopter pilot named Brett Wilson, who was already dressed in a dark blue flight suit with the gold-and-white Texas Law logo on his breast pocket. Once the search party found the bodies, Brett would collect them and fly them back to the complex after Michael O'Brien, the forensic pathologist who was also in attendance, conducted the initial autopsies.

Finally, Ryan said, "This is Hannah Jefferies."

She nodded toward her dog. While running her fingers over her dog's head, leaving furrows in the fur, she said, "This is Gypsum. We'll be helping with the search. We're new to the area but have worked search and rescue with law enforcement in the Dallas area."

She glanced up. Bruce, the man with the cowboy

hat and piercing blue eyes, was watching her. It was more than the striking color that made him interesting. It was his dark brow. His chiseled chin, covered with a sprinkling of gray hair. His shoulders were broad. The muscles of his chest were well-defined—even under his T-shirt.

Hannah wasn't looking for husband number three. But she was also a red-blooded American woman who liked the company of a good-looking man.

With a shake of her head, she looked away. Hannah couldn't get distracted by Bruce. Not when they were searching for someone as dangerous and deadly as Decker Newcombe.

Not when it might be their own lives on the line.

Chapter 3

Hannah sat on the back bench seat of a large SUV. Gypsum lay beside her, resting her head on Hannah's knee. She stroked the dog's silky ear and glanced around the vehicle. Gear for five people had been stowed in backpacks and rucksacks and placed in the cargo area. The windows were tinted dark and it looked like it was early evening outside and not mid-morning. The dashboard was sleek and surrounded by polished wood. The seats were covered in leather and buttery soft.

Trey was the driver, with Bruce riding shotgun and acting as the navigator. Slade and Ezra sat in the middle row of captain's chairs. Hannah didn't mind being relegated to the back seat. In fact, it made sense. She was the shortest of the bunch and didn't need as much leg room as the others. The bench seat also made it possible for Gypsum to stretch out at her side. She was happy that the dog was able to rest. The next few days would be grueling for everyone.

From where she sat, she had the perfect view of Bruce's profile. For the ride, he'd removed his hat, and he used the bend of his knee as a hook. Without the Stetson, she could see him properly. Her initial assessment was correct. He was handsome—especially with those aqua-colored eyes of his.

Sure, she'd decided not to be distracted by the handsome cowboy. But she couldn't help herself and wondered about his story. His body held some clues, and she read him like a book.

There was a ridge on his nose—a sure sign that it had been broken and not properly set. But what had caused the break? A fight? An accident? His neck was red with a sunburn. A white scar ran across the scarlet flesh from hairline to collar. The back of his neck was an odd place for a cut. Did it happen at the same time as the broken nose?

His left hand rested on the top of his hat.

He didn't wear a wedding band.

Although, the lack of a ring might not mean a thing.

He might be in a relationship but not married.

He might have a wife but not wear a ring because he worked with his hands all day.

Or he might not wear his ring because he was like her first husband—a cheating bastard.

Shifting in his seat, he turned to look over his shoulder. Their gazes met and held. Hannah gave him a tight-lipped smile. Bruce regarded her for a moment before facing forward.

Her cheeks flamed, red and hot. If it wasn't for her embarrassment, she would have thought it was another hot flash. First, she'd been caught watching Bruce. Then, he wouldn't even acknowledge her smile.

Well, it was probably all for the best. Hannah wasn't looking for Mr. Right or even Mr. Right Now.

Maybe she shouldn't have come on the search.

In her estimation, the younger trio of operatives was what happened when GI Joe was crossed with a boy band. She saw Bruce as the only ally in war between youth and experience. But it seemed like he wasn't interested in being friendly.

Bending to her dog, she kissed the top of her head. Hannah was rewarded with a lick to the face. She rubbed the canine's neck. At least Gypsum loved her.

Bruce was in the passenger seat of the large SUV, his heart hammering against his ribs. The vehicle had left the paved road. For several miles, they'd been driving down a dusty road that led to the heart of Hill Country to find a killer.

Only one thing worried him, and it wasn't Decker Newcombe. Why had he turned in his seat to spy on Hannah? And when she'd caught him looking and smiled, why hadn't he smiled back?

Good Lord, she must think he was a fool.

He could still feel Hannah's gaze on his neck, her look caressing him like a lover's touch. Unquestionably, she was the same person his daughter had mentioned that he should meet. What's more, Shana had been right. Hannah was perfect for him. At least, she seemed like the kind of woman he should want to meet—if he wanted to meet a woman to date, that is.

But he definitely did not want to get involved with anyone—not now and maybe not ever. Loving someone other than his wife felt like a betrayal of her memory. His chest tightened, squeezing his heart. He tried to bring Pamela's face to mind. It had been years since she died and, just like an old photograph, memories of her were starting to fade.

He stared out the window, watching the land unfurl like a rust-colored carpet. The sky was a deep shade of blue. Twisted oak trees, their leaves dull from the heat, dotted the landscape. He tried to concentrate on his mission, because he didn't want to think about Hannah or her deep brown eyes that were the same color as chocolate. Or her dark hair that was streaked with gray, making her look wise, confident and sexy. He definitely didn't want to think about her mouth, the same color as berries in the summer. Nor did he want to wonder if her kisses tasted as sweet as her lips looked.

And yet, he really couldn't think of anything else.

Turning in his seat again, he glanced at Hannah.

She was looking out the side window, stroking her dog's coat. It gave him a moment to study her more. He'd noticed her eyes and her hair and her mouth. But there was more about her looks to admire. She had long lashes and crinkles at the corners of her eyes. It told him that she was someone who spent time outdoors—just like him. It also told him that she liked to smile, something he hadn't done for years. She wore a loose tank top and jeans. The neck of her shirt was scooped low, accentuating her cleavage at the neckline. There were cords of muscles on her forearms. Her biceps and triceps were well defined. His fingers itched with the need to touch her.

Bruce balled his hand into a fist and faced forward again. He looked out the window. In the distance, a rock formation towered above all the others. Ghost Horse Point.

A sour taste filled his mouth as he realized his mistake.

"Crap." Even to Bruce's ears, the single word rang out like a shot.

From the driver's seat, Trey glanced in his direction. "What's wrong?"

"We missed the turn. It's back about a quarter mile."

"A quarter mile?" Trey repeated. His tone was filled with annoyance. "How'd we miss it by so much?"

It went without saying that Trey had an impressive résumé. He'd served in the 101st Airborne Division for eight years and had led troops into battle. More than once, he'd received medals and commendations. But it was also true that the younger man was a cocky son of a bitch. Bruce wasn't sure how the group of five would become a cohesive team. But they'd need to work together if they were going to find Decker and come out of the Texas wilderness alive.

That meant something else, too.

He had to focus on finding the killer.

"What do you know about Decker?" Slade asked, as if he knew that Bruce needed something other than Hannah to occupy his thoughts. "I mean, we were all briefed, but you've been living here. There has to be stuff you know that we don't."

It was a good question and for a moment, Bruce had nothing to say. "He's ruthless. Determined. He'll exploit any weakness and use it against you. The woman who owns the ranch I manage had a run-in with him a year or so back. Decker followed her boyfriend from all the way from San Antonio. During a storm, he cut the power to the house and snuck inside. Everyone survived, but Michael, her boyfriend, was hurt. Decker got swept away in the creek and we all hoped he died then, but he didn't."

"Is it true that Decker's related to Jack the Ripper? I heard something about that on a podcast. But it seems like something people make up to get listeners," said Ezra.

"I was wondering the same thing," said Trey as he drove.

"According to Ryan," said Hannah. "That's a fact. DNA was found on one of the Ripper's victims and it was linked back to Decker."

"Did Ryan say why Decker did what he does," asked Ezra. "I should've asked in the briefing…"

Hannah said, "He wants to be famous. A bigger name in killing than Jack the Ripper."

"So that means if we stop him, we'll be famous, too," said Slade with a laugh.

"We aren't here for the fame. We're here to do a job. Decker is dangerous. His ancestors don't matter," Trey admonished.

"It was a joke, man. I was kidding," Slade grumbled.

The conversation seemed to be over. Turning in his seat, he glanced at Hannah again.

He tried to reach for the grief he'd been carrying around for seven years since his wife's death. The emotions were like an old suitcase that had been stored in his heart instead of shoved beneath a bed. Every now and again, Bruce would stub his toe on the sadness and everything he'd kept stowed away for years would come out. This time, the grief was still there but the burden seemed lighter.

"Chill, man," said Slade. He brushed his long blond hair back from his forehead. Even if Bruce hadn't been told that the other man was from San Diego, he would've known he was a California native. His limbs were loose, and it seemed like nothing ever bothered him. "Everything out here looks exactly the same."

Ezra, the third Texas Law operative, remained silent. Maybe he didn't like conflict. Or maybe he just kept his thoughts to himself. Both were traits Bruce admired and possessed.

Muttering curses, Trey turned the SUV in a wide circle. A cloud of dust rose around the vehicle. As the grit settled, he started driving back the way they'd just come.

Leaning forward in his seat, Bruce stared out the windshield. Ten yards ahead was a break in the scrub brush that lined the roadside.

"There." He pointed. "On the left."

"See," said Slade. "That's easy to miss."

"Yeah." Trey let his foot off the accelerator and the SUV slowed. "But this guy's our guide. He's supposed to know where we're going."

"He figured pretty quick that we'd passed the turn. Sounds like he's doing a damn good job already."

Trey eased the SUV onto a narrow track. "Whatever."

"All right, boys." Hannah raised her voice to be heard from the back seat. "You two need to knock it off or I'll put you in time-out."

"Who do you think you are?" Trey asked. "My mom or something?"

"It seems like someone needs to be in charge. So, if you want to think of me as your mother, go ahead. But knock off the bickering."

Slade clapped a hand on Bruce's shoulder. "If Hannah's our mom, does that make you our dad?"

Bruce chuckled. Maybe it would be okay if he joined in the banter. Maybe humor was how they'd all connect. "Your mom's right. If you boys don't start behaving, there will be no dessert after dinner."

"Oh, man." Slade feigned disappointment. "I was looking forward to some melted ice cream."

Ezra chuckled. "Melted ice cream might be okay after walking in this heat. I've eaten worse."

"You can say that again," said Trey with a laugh.

It seemed like Hannah had the power to bring them all together. Once more, he looked over his shoulder and glanced at Hannah. She looked in his direction. Their eyes met. She smiled. This time, he couldn't help himself. The corners of his mouth rose, and Bruce smiled in return.

While Hannah had been in the offices of Texas Law, she had listened to the plan. In theory, it was simple. After driving to a little-used trailhead, the team would hike toward the campsite where the slaughter of the campers had occurred. Once they found the site, evidence would be collected. With that task finished, the helicopter would be contacted via satellite phone. Since there was no place to land, stretchers would be lowered, and the corpses would be pulled up by a winch.

The team was deliberately small. If a platoon of law enforcement officers came into the wilderness, the killer would know. The helicopter would be hard to miss—but it was the only way to retrieve the bodies they were also tasked with recovering. There were too many places in the hills for Decker to hide and, once again, he would disappear.

After that, she and Gypsum would do what they did best. They'd find the elusive killer, who was desperate and dangerous. That's when the trio from Texas Law would arrest Decker Newcombe and bring him to justice.

So, yeah, the job seemed straightforward. But as she exited the SUV and scanned the trail they were supposed to take, Hannah knew she'd been mistaken. The task was far from easy.

Trey stood next to the open liftgate, a backpack in each hand. "I think this is yours, Hannah," he said, holding out her pack.

She drew in a deep breath. It was like inhaling at the exact moment an oven door was open. She swallowed, soothing her dry and raw throat. Grabbing one of the shoulder straps, she said, "Thanks."

The SUV cast a narrow shadow on the ground. Gypsum ambled into the shade and flopped onto her belly.

Hannah spent a minute slathering sunscreen on her nose, cheeks and neck. She also donned a long-sleeved shirt with SPF 50 woven into the fibers. The last thing she wanted to worry about while in the field was a bad sunburn. Finally, she pulled a baseball cap low onto her brow.

Once she was done, Hannah placed her sunscreen into a side pocket. Hefting the bag onto her back, she tightened the chest and belly straps.

All the other team members adjusted their gear. The three operatives were dressed alike in khaki-colored cargo pants and T-shirts. Trey carried a semiautomatic with a long magazine that stuck from the butt end of the rifle. He also wore handguns in holsters on his hip, shoulder and thigh. She supposed that his job was security, along with being the team's leader. But all the other men were armed, as well. Ezra and Slade each wore handguns in holsters. Bruce had a shotgun that was strapped to the top of his pack. Hannah knew how to use a firearm. She just didn't carry one with her job. It was hard enough to handle a trained dog without worrying about accidentally shooting someone or something. For this job, she had a small Springfield Armory Hellcat tucked into her pack.

Bruce pointed toward a narrow track of dirt that wound up a hill before disappearing over the other side. "Ghost Horse Point is about five miles that way. The trail leads to a series of canyons. Good news. Once we reach the canyons, we'll have some shade and a break from the heat. It's predicted to get above a hundred and ten out here today, so the shade will be welcome. The bad news is there's no cellular coverage. Once we get over that ridge, we're on our own. Any questions?"

Trey shook his head. "No questions."

"I'm good," said Slade.

Ezra said, "Same."

Hannah had been on searches in difficult conditions before. Maybe not this difficult, but still… "I'm ready."

"Stay hydrated," Trey warned. "But conserve your water. The chopper will drop supplies and things we'll need when we make camp. But for now, all we have is what we're carrying."

"Stay hydrated and conserve water," said Slade. The corner of his mouth quirked into a smile, so she anticipated the joke even before he delivered the punch line. "Sounds like an oxymoron to me."

"The only moron around here is you," said Trey.

She wasn't sure if he was joking or not.

"Good one," said Slade with a laugh.

Trey started up the trail. Everyone fell in line behind him. Casting a glance over his shoulder, he said, "If you thought that was funny, wait until you hear all my 'your momma' jokes."

"You can't pick on my mom," said Ezra. "Remember, Hannah's everyone's mother."

"I'm far too young and good-looking to have birthed any one of you three," she said.

Her remark was followed by laughter.

Trey's rifle was attached to a strap that he'd slung over one shoulder and the opposite hip. Still, he carried the firearm across his chest, ready for any trouble. Next in line was Slade. His pack was loaded with the satellite phone and many of their provisions. Ezra came next, carrying what he'd need to conduct a forensic investigation, including a high-resolution camera, small flags on sticks, and evidence bags. She followed Ezra. Bruce was at the rear. He also carried his gun, in case anything—or make that, anyone—dangerous came up from behind.

The path cut across a wide field and then started to climb the hill. During the ascent, the conversation ceased. Hannah wasn't sure why the talking had stopped. Was it because everyone was conserving their breath? Or was it because Decker Newcombe could be anywhere?

Finally, they reached the summit. Hannah's legs ached. Her pulse hammered at the base of her skull. Her mouth was dry and sweat dampened her back. She glanced over the rise. The pitch down was as steep as it had been coming up. Sure, it'd be easier on her heart and lungs, but it would be killer on her knees. Then the land stretched out for several hundred yards before dropping into a warren of canyons.

"We made good time," said Trey. "Let's rest here for a minute."

Hannah unbuckled the straps of her backpack before letting it fall to the ground. She pressed her chest forward, easing away some of the tension. Then she knelt in the dirt and unfastened the zipper. From inside, she removed a collapsible bowl and plastic bladder with water. She filled the bowl, placing it in front of Gypsum so the dog could get a drink.

"You want some water?"

She looked up. Bruce stood beside her, holding out a dented canteen. The sun hit him from behind, surrounding him in a brilliant halo. With the light at his back, his features were shrouded in the shadow thrown by his cowboy hat; except for his blue eyes, that is.

Her heart skipped a beat. This time, it had nothing to

do with the climb. There was nothing wrong with being attracted to a handsome man, even if she didn't want a relationship. But she couldn't get caught up in the temptation, not with a killer on the loose.

"Thanks," she said, reaching for the canteen. Her hand brushed the back of his hand. Her palm warmed as a current of electricity danced along her skin.

Bruce sucked in a breath.

Or had she imagined that?

She took a sip of water, shaking off the unexpected feeling. Holding up the canteen, she said, "Thanks."

Taking back the flask, he replaced the top. "Any time."

Gypsum had slurped all but a few drops of water—a sure sign that she'd had enough. Hannah flattened the bowl before storing it in a front pocket of her bag. She rose to her feet. Bruce still stood at her side.

She needed to say something. But what?

"So," she began, "I guess you've lived here for a while. I mean, to have the knowledge of the area to be our guide."

"I've been here my whole life." His South Texas accent was thick. The last word came out with extra syllables. *Lii-iiffe.*

She thought it was cute and bit her bottom lip to keep from smiling.

"You know my daughter," he said. "Shana, the veterinarian."

"Shana McDaniel. Of course, I should've guessed you were related because of your last name." Shana was actually the first person in town Hannah had met. She'd made it a point to stop by and introduce herself—hoping that a partnership with the local vet would help drum up some business.

And it had.

Ryan Steele had been referred to Hannah after visiting Shana's office.

"Your daughter is great, by the way. The best, really. She invited me to her book club last week. I'm not much of a reader. But the other members were so nice, I'll be back next month."

"As a kid, Shana always had her nose in a book." Bruce gave a wistful smile and shook his head. "I guess all the reading helped her become a veterinarian. After her schooling, she could've gone anywhere but came home on account of her mother." Pride was evident with each word spoken—until the end, that is. Then Bruce changed. He was like a house with all the shades drawn, hiding whatever was going on inside.

Before she could say anything else, Trey raised his hand into the air. He drew a circle in the sky with a finger. "Let's move out."

They headed into the canyons, walking single file. Bruce was first, followed by Slade. Hannah and Gypsum were next. Ezra walked behind her, and Trey took up the rear. The sheer walls rose up on both sides, blocking out most of the sun and some of the heat. The rock was striated, each layer representing a different era going back to when this land had been the bed of a prehistoric sea.

"It's not much farther now," said Bruce, his voice echoing off the canyon's walls.

Hannah should be focused on finding Decker Newcombe, but she kept wondering about Bruce. There was more to him than just being a ranch manager who'd lived in Mercy since birth. After several miles of walking, she still hadn't figured anything out.

That's when she heard a droning sound. It was like the far-off motor of a big rig or the engine of a nearby airplane. At her side, Gypsum whined and slowed her pace. "What is it, girl?"

"Yeah," asked Slade, "what is that noise? Did the helicopter find somewhere to land?"

"That's not an aircraft," said Ezra. "Those are flies."

The narrow passage opened to a wide plain. Like a single black cloud, insects buzzed just above the dirt. On the ground were three bloated masses of flesh and grizzle. Bile rose in the back of Hannah's throat. The scent of rotten bodies, like meat that had been left out in the sun, hung in the air. Pressing a hand to her mouth and nose, she covered the stench. At her side, Gypsum whined and took a step back. She didn't blame the dog. The smell of death was unmistakable. As was the fact that they'd found the place where Decker Newcombe had committed his latest massacre.

Chapter 4

The sun was high, a white ball in a sky of bright blue. Hannah and Gypsum sat in the narrow strip of shade and waited as Ezra and his fellow Texas Law operatives documented the crime scene. To clear away the flies, they'd ignited a smoke bomb. The air was filled with the acrid scent of manufactured fumes that burned her eyes and made her throat itch. The only blessing was that it covered much of the rotting stench of death.

Bruce approached. "How are you doing?"

Hannah had seen death more than once. After all, not every search and rescue had a happy ending. But she'd never seen anything like this before. "It's a lot to take in."

After dropping onto the hard-packed earth beside her, Bruce sighed. "It's a hell of a thing, that's for sure."

It seemed like Bruce was a master at understatements. But he was right about one thing: the scene looked like something straight from hell. "Do you know how much longer this will take?"

"Are you excited to go back to hiking in this heat?" Bruce was smiling, so she knew that he was joking.

He had a nice smile that filled his whole face and

crinkled the corners of his eyes. Despite their grisly surroundings, her pulse spiked.

She gave a soft laugh and shook her head. “I just want to get this job done.”

Pointing to the trio of operatives, Bruce said, “Ezra thinks he found something that belonged to Decker. Will Gypsum be able to get a scent?”

“Not to brag,” she said, eyeing the Lab at her side, “but she’s the best.”

“Hopefully, we will get this job done—once and for all.” Bruce stood. “Those guys are almost finished. Slade just called the helicopter. Once the aircraft has taken the bodies, we’ll be ready to go.”

Bruce was right. Several minutes later, a helicopter appeared on the horizon. The fuselage was white. Stenciled onto the tail rotor in blue-and-gold lettering was the Texas Law logo. Hannah waited. All three bodies were secured in body bags. Then, one at a time, each was placed on a stretcher and lifted into the helicopter.

Once all three corpses were loaded onto the chopper, supplies for the campsite were lowered using the same winch. There was a five-person tent. Sleeping bags for each member of the team. More food and water. And a camp stove, along with a small tank of propane for heat. At the end of the day, the team would set up their own campsite.

As the helicopter flew away, Ezra approached Hannah. He was carrying a brown paper bag. The word *Evidence* was stamped on the side. “We found this,” he said, holding out the bag to her. “It’s tattered and torn, and a smaller size than any of the victims wore. I think it belonged to Decker. Can your dog get a whiff and see if it leads her anywhere?"

"Let's find out." After rising to her feet, Hannah took the bag from Ezra and removed the T-shirt. At one time, it had been a typical man's undershirt. Now, the white cloth was gray with sweat and dirt. Holding out the garment to Gypsum, she waited for her dog to gain interest. The Lab sniffed, taking in the scent. Then Hannah gave the command. "Seek."

Gypsum paused a moment before pulling on the lead.

"She has something," said Hannah.

"That's our cue," said Trey. "Let's go."

Hannah trusted her dog and knew that Gypsum had picked up what she hoped was the killer's scent. The dog led them across a small valley and into another canyon. Sheer rock cliffs stood on either side of them, opening at the top to a bright blue sky. It would have been beautiful, except for the dangerous situation.

As the rock walls blotted out the sun, adrenaline filled her veins. Her hand trembled slightly, and she held tighter to the leash. Glancing once over her shoulder, she saw that the men were following her in a line. Trey was right behind her. His rifle was out and at the ready. Next came Bruce, also with his long gun. Ezra was next, holding his sidearm. Slade was last, and his gun was out, as well.

They'd been in the middle of Hill Country for hours already. After forty-five minutes of tracking, Gypsum began to whine.

"What is it, girl?"

The dog pulled to a spot where a prehistoric river had

cut two channels in the earth. One fork went left, the other to the right. Gypsum regarded both pathways and panted. Then, nose to the ground, she chose the right-hand side. From ten yards away, it was obvious what the canine had found.

A firepit had been dug into the ground. It was circled by stones and charred bits of wood were still stacked atop one another.

"Good girl." Hannah pulled a dog treat from a side pocket in her backpack. Holding out her hand, she let Gypsum lick the kibble from her palm. "You did it."

"Be careful, everyone," Trey warned. He looked up, air-tracing the ridgeline with the barrel of his rifle. "Decker could be anywhere."

His words sent a chill through Hannah. Wrapping her arms across her chest, she quelled a shiver. Bruce strode toward the firepit and knelt in the dirt. Holding his hand over the burnt logs, he said, "It's still warm and hasn't been out for long. Four or five hours. Six at the most."

"Surprisingly, it means Decker is close. Maybe he's hoping to find another group of campers and steal their gear and keys to a vehicle," said Ezra. "We need to call this in and get an aerial search going."

"I'm on it," said Slade, dropping his bag to the ground. He unzipped the backpack's main compartment and removed the satellite phone. To Hannah, it looked more like a red walkie-talkie than a smartphone. Slade turned a dial for a moment. Then his brows pulled together. "The cliffs are too high. We aren't getting a signal." Picking up his backpack, he slung a strap over his shoulder. "I'll hike back and find a signal."

"Are you sure that's best?" Hannah asked. "I mean, Ezra just said that Decker's nearby."

"Yeah," said Bruce. "If you're going back, we should all go with you."

Slade waved away their concern. "It won't take long to find a signal. This little beauty is really powerful. I'm surprised it's not working here. Besides, there might be more evidence to collect. Ezra can process this scene while I'm gone."

Hannah had been on enough search and rescues to know that Slade was right about the evidence, at least.

Trey, as team leader, was the one who made the final decision. "Ezra and I will see if Decker left anything behind that might tell us where he went or what he's going to do next."

"I'll be back once I get a signal," said Slade. "It won't take a minute."

Hannah watched the other man walk away. Once he passed the fork in the canyon's wall, he disappeared from view.

Gypsum sat and whined softly. Rubbing the dog's head, she said, "It's okay, girl. You did good."

At the same time, she felt the dog's anxiety. Hannah wouldn't feel better until Slade returned and the team was back together.

With the satellite phone in one hand and his Glock G17 in the other, Slade retraced his steps. He tried to keep his eyes everywhere at once: The canyon in front of him. The canyon at his back. The rim, where an ambush would be most effective. The screen of the satellite phone.

There was nothing to see other than dirt, rock, sky and a continual message that scrolled across the screen. *Acquiring Signal.* His eyes saw what his brain failed to register. After taking two steps, he stopped and turned around. There, about six feet above the ground, was a ledge. It wasn't much, but he only needed to gain a little height to link to the satellite.

Slade holstered his gun and then tucked the sat phone into a side pocket on his cargo pants. He reached for the ledge and hoisted himself up. Back pressed against the canyon wall, he removed the phone from his pocket and glanced at the screen. *Acquiring Signal.*

"Dammit."

He didn't want to hike all the way to the mouth of the canyon—a place he'd get a signal for sure. Then again, maybe he wouldn't have to. There was a narrow track that led all the way to the rim of the rock wall. At the top of the canyon, with nothing blocking the signal, he'd be able to place a call.

He slipped the phone back into his pocket and secured the flap closed. Then he reached for another handhold. He raised himself, placing his feet on a narrow ledge. He found another handhold and another one after that. Within minutes, he reached the rim of the canyon. At the top, he stood on a narrow strip of land. There was a sheer drop on either side. A few scraggy trees grew on the plateau. Another large rock formation formed a tower and threw a long shadow across the ground.

In front of him was a vista of red rocks, blue sky and

brown earth. There was a rugged beauty to the landscape, so different from his home in Southern California. Stepping to the edge, he looked down to see how far he'd climbed. By his estimation, it was fifty feet to the ground—maybe even more. The height left him dizzy.

Then again, it didn't matter. He was certainly high enough to catch a signal now. Pulling the phone from his pocket, he turned on the satellite phone. It immediately picked up a signal. He entered a series of numbers, and his finger hovered over the call button.

That's when he heard it.

There was a noise, like the whisper of a breath, and he glanced over his shoulder. Then, several small stones slid out from beneath his feet. Like wheels on a roller skate, they pulled him forward. Trying to keep his balance, he windmilled his arms and leaned back. It wasn't enough.

The blood in his veins turned icy. He tried to call out, but it was too late. He fell over the edge. For a moment, he was weightless. The ground was just a tiny speck before he hit the dirt. Every part of his body screamed in pain, and like a flash of lightning, his world was gone as quickly as it came.

Bruce McDaniel tried to be helpful to the operatives from Texas Law as they collected evidence. But honestly, the two men were professionals and there wasn't much to see. Aside from the remnants of a fire, there were holes in the ground that were consistent with tent pegs and a flattened surface where the tent itself had been pitched. Bruce guessed that Decker saw the helicopter. The killer would have assumed that people were looking for him, so he packed up and moved deeper into the hills.

Ezra busied himself with documenting the scene—taking pictures, drawing diagrams and marking objects with little flags. Trey spent time both looking for clues and complaining about how long Slade had been gone. For her part, Hannah sat in the shade. Panting, Gypsum lay at Hannah's feet.

Bruce knew there was nothing more he could do. Drawn to Hannah, he wandered over to where she sat. "Mind if I join you?"

She gave him a small smile. "Help yourself."

He lowered himself onto the ground and leaned against the canyon wall. The rock was warm and loosened the knots of muscles in his lower back. "They haven't found much," he said, as if she hadn't been sitting nearby and watching the whole time. "I tried to help, but there's just not much here."

She nodded slowly. "I've been out on plenty of these things before. The first thing I learned is to let the professionals do their jobs."

He didn't take her words as chastisement, but wisdom shared. Bruce nodded slowly. Usually, he was happy with his own company and the quiet. The silence sat between them like an uninvited guest. Sitting next to Hannah and saying nothing seemed like a waste. "You ever been on a search for a killer?"

She nodded. "There was this one man who shot up a convenience store, killing two people. Then he stole a car. The police found the vehicle a day later. It was parked in the middle of nowhere. Gypsum and I tracked him for miles before he was found."

"Did he put up a fight?"

Hannah paused and bit her bottom lip. The gesture was sexy as hell. Bruce dropped his eyes to the tips of his boots.

"You know, I don't remember," she said after a moment. "So, I guess it wasn't too much of a fight. Maybe he knew that he wasn't going to get away. Or maybe he knew that he wouldn't survive much longer on his own."

Bruce gave a small laugh, even though he wasn't sure that she had meant to be funny. After all, surviving in the harsh Texas wilderness was no joke. The dog started to whine. He held out his hand for Gypsum to sniff. "What is it, girl?"

Leaning forward, the canine snuffled his hand before lowering her head for him to give her a scratch. He ruffled the fur on top of her head. He still felt as if he should say something, but Hannah seemed fine with the quiet. As the seconds stretched out into minutes, Bruce recalled the last time he'd just sat with a woman. It had been on the porch, and with his wife. They hadn't yet known that she had cancer. In fact, his wife had felt fine and told him about her day as a fourth-grade teacher.

That was the last time Bruce had been happy, as well.

The memory stung his eyes. He blinked hard before glancing at Hannah. She wasn't looking in his direction. Thank God, she hadn't noticed him getting all misty. He followed her gaze. She watched the two Texas Law operatives. They stood near the remnant of the campfire. Both men leaned into each other, legs braced and shoulders squared.

"Looks like something's going on between those two," said Hannah.

She was right. "Yeah, but what are they arguing about?"

"I don't like that Slade's been gone this long," said Trey, speaking loud enough to be heard.

"He might've had to hike out of the canyon just to get a signal," said Ezra. "It took us forty-five minutes to get here. That means a round trip is ninety minutes, minimum. It's only been an hour. Give the guy some time."

As far as Bruce was concerned, both men were right. Hannah rose to her feet and walked to where the men were standing. "I'm with Trey," she said. "Slade shouldn't have gone off on his own. There's more out here that can hurt someone besides Decker Newcombe."

"What do you think, Bruce? You're our resident expert," said Ezra. "Should we go looking for Slade?"

"Hannah's right about this area being dangerous," he said, getting to his feet. "It's not uncommon to find four-foot rattlesnakes near the ranch. It would have enough venom to kill a child and make a grown man sick. If you're done collecting evidence, I say we double back."

"I get that this is a dangerous place," said Ezra. "But what happens if Slade comes back here and we're gone?"

Bruce had an answer. "If he retraced his steps, he's just heading out of the canyon. If he had to hike to the mouth to get service, he's already placed the call. That means he's coming in this direction. If we go back, we'll run across each other eventually."

"What if he took another fork?" asked Ezra.

"Slade isn't stupid," said Trey.

"I guess you're right." Ezra still held a camera. Picking up his backpack from the ground, he stowed the equipment in a compartment. "I'm done here. We can leave whenever you want."

Bruce removed a dented canteen from his own pack and took a long swallow. "Let's go."

For the trek out of the canyon, Bruce took point. He had his shotgun out, ready to use. Hannah and Gypsum followed. Ezra was next in line. Trey, armed with his rifle, was the sweep.

As they walked down the narrow chasm, Gypsum put her nose to the ground and pulled against the leash, sending Hannah off-balance. Bruce's fingers itched with the need to keep her upright and steady.

"What is it, Gypsum?" she asked, jogging to keep up with the dog. "Do you smell Decker Newcombe again?"

Bruce went cold, the sweat on his neck drying in an instant. Was the killer watching them even now? He scanned the ridgeline, looking for the outline of a man. The upper lip of the gorge was empty. But that didn't mean they were alone. He lifted the gun, tucking it between his elbow and ribs.

"Ezra," said Hannah, "do you still have that shirt?"

"Sure do." The operative stepped forward. Holding the evidence bag, he opened the top and held it in front of the dog. Gypsum stuck her nose inside the sack.

Then Hannah gave the dog a command. "Seek."

Gypsum began trotting, straining against the lead. She headed toward the entrance to the canyon. Hannah jogged behind the dog. Bruce jogged, too. He wasn't about to let Hannah out of his sight, not when the killer's scent was so close.

There was a bend in the canyon wall. Bruce had no idea what was on the other side. As far as he was concerned, it was the perfect place for an ambush. "Hold up," he said, reaching for Hannah's shoulder. She was more muscular than he would've guessed and yet her skin was soft. For a moment, he could only think of how nice it was to touch Hannah. But he shoved away the thought and refocused. "Let me go first. We don't know what we're walking into."

She regarded him with her large brown eyes. Bruce thought she was going to refuse. Or worse yet, accuse him of being sexist or having the sensibilities of a caveman. But she did none of those. Instead, she stepped aside. "You do have the gun."

Bruce could feel it in his bones; the killer was close. Ezra removed his own firearm, a black handgun, and held it out, ready to fire. Trey had his rifle out, as well. The team was ready. This was the moment that the nightmare would end, and Decker would be taken into custody.

Lifting the stock of his shotgun to his shoulder, Bruce stared down the barrel. Keeping his back pressed to the rock wall, he shuffled forward. Hannah and her dog were a few steps back. The operatives from Texas Law were behind her. He took one step forward and then another. Bruce's shoulders were tight. His heart thumped against his chest, sending his pulse racing. His own breaths were loud in his ears. Whatever waited for them on the other side of the bend was only a few paces away.

Inhaling deeply, he stepped forward.

Then, he stopped in his tracks.

Lying on the ground was Slade. His head was turned at an unnatural angle. Blood oozed from his nose, mouth and ears. It collected into a pool of gore. One strap of his backpack was looped over his shoulder. The guts and casing of the satellite phone were scattered around his outstretched hand. His eyes were open, staring at nothing.

Behind Bruce, Hannah swallowed hard. "Slade is dead."

Chapter 5

Hannah had seen corpses before. But this one hit her differently. Every part of her body ached, and it was hard to breathe.

Gypsum plopped her butt onto the ground. It was her way of signaling that she'd found what she was seeking. Slade's corpse must've been what got the dog agitated. Pulling a handful of kibbles from her pocket, she held out her palm to Gypsum. "Good dog," she said to the canine. Then, to the others, she asked, "What happened to him?"

"Aside from the fact that he broke his neck, you mean?" asked Ezra.

Trey stood next to the body and looked up. "I think he climbed to the top to get a signal and then fell." He pointed upward. "There on the rim, you can see skid marks from here."

He was right. There were several white slashes on the red stone. Several small rocks surrounded the body. It was as if he had stood at the edge and lost his footing. Or maybe the brittle sandstone had given way.

Bruce muttered a curse. "It looks like an accident to me."

Hannah had come across bodies of other people who'd fallen to their deaths before. "Yeah, but how did he get up there?"

Trey placed his hand on the canyon wall. "There's a ledge right there," he said, indicating a narrow outcropping of rock. "I think there are handholds all the way to the top. This wall is definitely climbable—even without equipment."

Ezra knelt next to the body and pulled Slade's eyes closed. "What do we do now?"

"We have to call this in." Trey touched a piece of the satellite phone with the toe of his hiking boot. "But we're going to have to get cellular coverage."

"We won't get much of that out here," said Bruce. "We need to start heading back, but I'm not sure how much ground we'll cover before it gets too dark to see."

She checked her watch. It was almost 4:30 p.m. It had been hours since they'd left the Texas Law offices in Mercy. It would take them hours more to get back to the vehicle. It meant that Bruce was right. They'd lose the daylight long before they reached the car. That brought up another problem.

"We can't just leave Slade here," said Hannah. Sure, she hadn't known him long, but she knew that he deserved better than to be left for wild animals to pick at his bones.

"We aren't going to leave him." Trey dropped his pack onto the ground. From inside, he removed a tarp. "Help me roll him onto this and we'll use it as a stretcher to carry him out."

Slade was placed at the edge of the sheeting. Ezra

and Trey took time to tuck the plastic around the corpse. Then the body was flipped back to front until it was wrapped in the shroud.

She stood to the side, watching as the operatives worked. Her eyes stung with tears she refused to cry. Her face warmed, the heat radiating outward until it consumed her chest, her belly and her scalp.

Damn. Hot flash.

"Are you okay?" Bruce asked, placing his calloused palm on her shoulder. Far from being put off by the hardened touch, she was drawn by his concern and appreciated the gesture.

His question still hung between them. Was she okay?

Well, she was in the wilderness and having a hot flash. Aside from her unruly hormones, one of their teammates had fallen to his death. They'd also lost their best way to contact the outside world. It was impossible to keep the dark thoughts at bay. She'd been too hasty in accepting the job. "I'm in shock, I guess."

"We all are." He held up his dented canteen. "You need a drink? It'll help."

Hannah pulled a bottle of water from her own pack. "I've got some," she said while unscrewing the top.

She placed the rim to her lips and let cool water slide down her throat. Then she poured a small amount of water into her cupped hand and splashed her face and chest. The hot flash began to fade.

"Let's go," said Trey. "The quicker we get out of here, the quicker we can find a cellular signal and call Texas Law."

The ends of the shroud were carried by Ezra and Trey.

Bruce was at the head of the line, his shotgun still out and ready. Next came the two operatives and the body of their compatriot. Hannah was at the rear. Ezra had given her his firearm—just in case—and it was stowed in the webbing of her backpack. She also carried Slade's pack on her chest.

The quartet walked without talking. This time, the silence wasn't for stealth. They were somber over the loss of Slade. By the time they reached the mouth of the canyon and the place where they'd left their gear, the sun hung low on the western horizon. They set the body next to a large boulder that was several yards outside the camp. Hannah placed Slade's bag next to all the supplies the helicopter had dropped earlier in the day.

"I know this has been rough for everyone," said Trey. "But I think that we shouldn't take any more chances. I say we set up camp for the night, get something to eat, and in the morning, we can find a way to call all this in."

To Hannah, it sounded like the best idea. "Agreed."

"Ditto," said Ezra.

"I hate to be the fly in the ointment," said Bruce, "but Slade's body is going to attract animals. If we don't want to spend the night fighting off packs of wild dogs and such, we have to do something with him."

Trey asked, "What do you have in mind?"

"We can bury him in a shallow grave." He dug the toe of his boot into the dirt, scuffing away a few pebbles. "But the ground is pretty hard. I suggest that we pile rocks on top of him."

Trey looked to his left and right, seeming to survey his surroundings. "Rocks we have. I think that Bruce's idea is best. Everyone, collect all the stones you can carry. Remember that snakes hide under the rocks, and they might not be happy to have their homes disturbed."

Hannah doubted that anyone in the group needed the reminder. Several varieties of venomous snakes lived in the area. There were also scorpions and tarantulas. Yet she appreciated that Trey was being thorough. She nodded once before wandering away to collect whatever stones she could find. The rest of the group dispersed. Bruce walked in her direction. Was he following her? Well, if he was, she didn't mind.

"Hell of a thing," he said. "It feels like this search is cursed."

Without looking at Bruce, she asked, "You think a deity knocked Slade off that cliff?"

Sure, she was being hyperbolic. But at the same time, she was curious about Bruce's thinking.

"Nah, that was just an accident." Picking up a stick from the ground, he poked at the base of a stone. "There's nothing under this one."

"Why'd you say this search was cursed?" she asked, slipping the loop of Gypsum's lead around her wrist. Then Hannah bent and picked up the stone. It was heavier than she'd expected. The weight pulled at her shoulders and lower back. "To be honest, I don't see you as a superstitious kind of person."

"I'm not superstitious, either. It's just that nothing is going our way." He picked up his own rock. Together, they carried them to where Slade's body was still wrapped in the tarp. "But I'm a realist. Losing someone within a few hours of getting started is bad. The fact that we can't make a call is also bad. It makes me wonder what else will go wrong."

"I hope nothing else goes wrong," she said, setting her rock on a pile next to the body. At the same time, she knew that hope was a wasted emotion. Next to her, Gypsum panted. "There's no reason to drag my dog around in this heat. I'm going to get her settled somewhere."

"The dog has been a hell of a team member," he said. "Let her get some rest."

A large boulder threw shade across the ground. From her pack, Hannah removed a metal stake and the collapsible water dish. After driving the stake into the ground, she attached the dog's lead and filled the bowl with water. Petting the dog's head, she ordered, "Stay."

Gypsum lapped the water and dropped onto her side.

By the time all the rocks around the camp were piled next to the shroud, the sun had dipped to meet the horizon. Trey, Ezra and Bruce had been efficient in collecting what they'd needed. Now there was nothing left to do but cover up Slade.

As the sun slipped below the horizon, the last stone was placed on the body.

"Should we say something?" Hannah asked. Dusk had fallen, and the sky was a brilliant shade of purple with pink at the edges. "I don't know if he was religious or not, but it seems like we should give his memory a few words."

Trey asked, "Bruce, you want to do the honors?"

Bruce removed his hat. The band had left an indentation on his hair. Holding the brim, he lowered his gaze. "Slade was a good man," he began. "I didn't know him well or for long, but there were a few things about him that I learned. He was dedicated to his job. He had a good sense of humor and always found the positive in any situation. I know those are rare qualities in a person and the world is a dimmer place without his sunny disposition. I hope that whatever waits for him on the other side of this life treats him well."

Hannah was like Bruce; she had only known Slade for a few hours. Yet the loss of life—and a young, vibrant one at that—was a fist to the chest. "Thank you," she said, wiping her eyes with her shoulder. "That was nice."

"Thanks, man," said Ezra. "I think he'd appreciate what you had to say."

Trey clapped his hand on Bruce's shoulder. "Good job." And then he asked, "Where did Slade's bag get dropped?"

Ezra nodded toward the pile of gear. "It's over there with all the stuff. His is the blue one. But what do you need it for?"

"I don't want to sound insensitive or anything…" said Trey as he picked up Slade's backpack. "But I want to make sure that we have his Glock."

He began rummaging through the bag. Ezra peered over his shoulder.

Dusk was slowly turning to night. The sky had turned from purple to indigo and already a few stars were visible. To Hannah, it was obvious that the operatives from Texas Law were preoccupied with the misplaced firearm. But there was more to be done than just finding the gun. "We should set up the tent with what light we have left," she said to Bruce.

Bruce brought over the nylon sack. For a few moments, they unpacked the contents in silence. Stakes. Poles. Tent.

"This reminds me of taking Shana camping when she was little." He smiled while assembling the poles, his voice taking on a wistful tone. "Just me, Shana and her mom. We'd take a tent and a cooler and head out to the Hill Country. Hike. Cook over a fire. Tell stories under the stars."

Despite the recent death, Bruce's happy reminiscences made Hannah smile. "Sounds like nice memories you made with your family." She laid out the tent on a flat piece of ground that was free of rocks.

"They are nice memories," he said, handing Hannah several metal stakes.

Her fingertips brushed the back of his hand. That same electric charge as before surged up her arm. Her heartbeat raced. Like before, she heard his sharp inhale.

She raised her gaze. He was watching her. In the dusk and under the shadow of his hat's brim, she could see his piercing blue eyes. This was not the time to find a man attractive. But she couldn't help herself. Despite the fact that she wasn't looking for romance, Bruce McDaniel was everything she should want. Handsome. Resourceful. Smart.

He took a step toward her. She couldn't stop the connection if she wanted. She closed the distance between them. He rubbed his thumb on the back of her wrist. And just as quickly, Bruce jerked his hand away, as if he'd been scalded. The stakes tumbled to the ground.

Hannah's face flamed red and hot with embarrassment.

"Crap," he muttered. Bending down, he collected the stakes. "I'll get these into the ground," he said. "You can start threading the frame through the grommets."

"I'm going to check on Gypsum." It was an excuse. She needed some distance from Bruce.

The canine lay on her side and looked up as Hannah approached. Taking a knee, she ran her fingers through the dog's fur. "How's it going? You need more water?"

There was a little bit of liquid in the bottom of the bowl. At least Gypsum wasn't dehydrated. Still, she poured more water into the dish. Rubbing the nape of the dog's neck, she took in a long breath and let it out slowly.

Obviously, she and Bruce had a physical attraction. But just as obviously, it was something he didn't want. Disappointment sat in her belly like a rock. Then again, she'd moved to Mercy to start over—and that meant leaving bad habits behind. Like desiring men who weren't right for her.

There were other things for Hannah to worry about—like the fact that Decker was out there, somewhere. Maybe he was watching them now. Slade's death bothered Hannah more than she let on. What if his fall wasn't an accident? With a killer on the loose, everyone had to stay vigilant.

Oh sure, Bruce McDaniel seemed like a nice enough guy. But she didn't want to get involved with anyone. Besides, if he didn't want a relationship with her, there was no reason to want him.

Bruce swung the hammer hard. It hit the metal stake with the peal of a broken bell. He hit it again and again.

It did nothing to relieve his frustration. He shouldn't be attracted to Hannah—and yet he was. Being close to her was difficult. But touching her was a special kind of torture.

It had been years since he'd had any romantic inclination for a woman, and finding Hannah was like being run over by a truck.

His eyes traveled to where Hannah sat on the ground with her dog. Gypsum seemed just fine to him, wagging her tail and getting pets. Was checking on the dog just an excuse to get away from him? Well, if it was, he didn't blame her. Once again, he'd made a mess. He needed to fix it. But how?

Before he could think of anything to say or do, Trey rose from where he'd scattered Slade's belongings on the ground. He stalked over to where the body had been covered with rocks. Picking a stone from atop the pile, he threw it to the side.

Ezra chased after him. "Dude. What in the hell? You can't unbury him. That's sacrilegious."

Bruce was on his feet before he realized that he was standing. Striding to the temporary grave, he called out, "What's going on?"

Hannah held tight to Gypsum's lead and followed. "What are you doing, Trey?"

Ezra answered, "We can't find Slade's gun. It's not in his bag. Trey wants to see if we somehow buried him with the Glock."

"I don't remember seeing a gun on him." Bruce brought back that horrible moment when they'd discovered the body. The broken phone. The eyes, staring at nothing. The pool of blood on the ground. "I mean, I didn't look closely before we wrapped him in the tarp …"

"That's what I said," said Ezra, setting the discarded rock back in place.

"Don't you all get it?" asked Trey, narrowing his eyes. "If Slade doesn't have his gun in his bag and it's not on him—then where is it?"

"Must've fallen out of his holster when he slipped," said Hannah.

Bruce nodded. "That makes sense to me."

"Then why wasn't it on the ground, next to his body? We found the phone."

"You saw that rock wall." Bruce knew that Hannah had landed on the most reasonable explanation. "There were ledges and handholds all the way to the top. That gun could've landed on any one of them. If it did, then it's still there now."

Trey regarded him, his eyes still narrowed. Then he slowly shook his head. "Could be, man," he said. "Could be. I should go and check." He turned and took two steps toward the canyon.

Bruce grabbed Trey by the shoulder, spinning the younger man around so they were nose to nose. "It's too dark," he said. "You can't go back and try to climb that wall if there isn't any light—not unless you have another tarp for us to wrap around your body."

"We can't just leave that gun out there," said Trey.

"It's not going to grow legs and walk away," said Bruce, knowing full well that he was being sarcastic. The thing was, Trey was being unreasonable.

"I'm not worried about the gun itself," said Trey. "But

what if Decker finds it first? We can't have a killer on the loose with a fully loaded firearm."

"There's also the possibility that Decker already has the gun," said Ezra. "Face it, he could have pushed Slade off the cliff."

Folding her arms over her chest, Hannah shivered. True, she'd worried about that already. But hearing Ezra say the words made the possibility all too real. "Do you think that's what happened?"

"As a cop, I always kept an open mind. Decker killing Slade is a possibility. That's all I'm saying."

It was Bruce's turn to nod slowly as the truth settled on him. "You're right, we can't just leave Slade's gun laying around for someone—make that Decker Newcombe—to find. But we also can't go looking for it right now, either." He paused. "Besides, we can't split up. First thing in the morning, we'll go back and look for the gun. Then, we'll find a signal and place a call."

"All that hiking will take hours—time we don't have," said Trey. "We need to break into two teams. One to go after the gun. The other to call Texas Law."

"The last thing we want is people to get lost. You know how many resources that'll waste?" asked Hannah.

"I won't get lost," said Trey. "I was taught land navigation in the army. Besides, we've been to the canyon before. I can find my way there and back."

Ezra shrugged. Bruce assumed that meant he agreed.

Still, he wasn't going to let Trey and Ezra wander away from camp in the dark. "It stands to reason that if we can't find the firearm right now, then neither can anyone else."

"That makes sense to me," said Hannah. "Although, what do we do if Decker did push Slade off the cliff?"

"Our jobs," said Bruce. "Nothing changes."

"You're right," she said, giving him a small smile.

True, he didn't need her—or anyone else—to agree with his ideas. But hearing Hannah say that she thought he was right filled his chest with pride. Glancing at her, he nodded his thanks. She gave him that same smile again and hope swirled through the pride. Maybe he hadn't messed up with her as much as he'd feared.

Bruce continued with a plan. "I say we break up at first light. Hannah and I will look for a cellular signal." After all, he knew the area best. "You and Ezra find the gun. We can hopefully get both done before it gets too hot."

"Sounds like the best tactic," Trey said before speaking to Bruce directly. "You want to help me start a fire and get some grub cooking? Hannah and Ezra can finish setting up the tent."

Bruce wanted time alone with Hannah so he could… what?

He wasn't about to explain himself to her. He barely knew her, and besides, what was he going to say?

I think you're really pretty. And I like the way your skin feels whenever I touch you. And I like the way you smell and think and laugh. But there's no future for us because of my wife—who happened to die years ago.

No. He'd sound like a bigger fool than he acted. Best to just let her work with Ezra while he got some dinner started.

"C'mon," he said to Trey. "Let's see what food was air-dropped to us."

Trey set a pair of battery-operated camp lights on the ground. It gave them enough light to search through a cardboard box. Inside, they found military-style MREs. There were several dinner varieties: pasta, pork and beans, and barbecue chicken with rice. There was also applesauce, oatmeal and peaches. Bruce wasn't sure how the heavily processed meals would taste, but it was better than nothing.

Bruce began to sort the foodstuffs into piles. Breakfast. Lunch. Dinner. On-the-go snacks. While he sorted the food, he glanced at Hannah. Ezra was holding the flashlight as she snaked the tent frame through the grommets. Gypsum lay at her side, head on paws, lazily inspecting the construction. His heart squeezed in his chest. He didn't know what to do with his new feelings and he shoved away the emotions.

Standing tall, Bruce placed his hands on his lower back and pressed forward with his chest. His tight muscles stretched and loosened. Night had fallen, turning the landscape an inky black. Anything—or anyone—could be lurking in the dark. He hoped that in the morning they'd find Slade's gun, just as Hannah had suggested. But if that was the case, why was there an uneasy feeling in the pit of his stomach? And where was Decker Newcombe at this very moment?

Chapter 6

Decker lay on his stomach and stared through a pair of binoculars. The stolen spyglasses had belonged to one of the guys he'd killed a few days earlier. Which one of the three? He didn't know.

What he did know was that one of the campers had gotten away. He'd hoped that the guy had gotten lost and died, but all that hope had been for nothing. Obviously, the dude had survived and somehow made it to civilization.

Now, there was a manhunt. Once again, Decker was the target.

Through the binoculars, he focused on the newest campsite. There were four people—three male and one female. There was also a tracking dog. He'd seen enough to know that each and every one of the people was armed. They were also professionals.

It was more than the helicopter that had picked up the remains from his latest slaughter. Or that the same helicopter had delivered supplies. The woman and her dog stood atop a large rock, giving her the perfect view of the area as she held watch.

How long could he expect to stay the hunter when he

was also being hunted? He only had a few more days of food and water left. He couldn't start a fire without the team of operatives—never mind that dog—catching the scent. He'd wasted all his bullets shooting at a guy who'd escaped anyway. Even if he got out of the wilderness alive, where was he supposed to go? There was nobody left for him to call. No place left for him to get help.

Decker's chest started to burn, like he'd swallowed acid.

Well, he'd been on his own before. He could handle it again. He'd also been considered the underdog more than once and always come out on top. Like the first time he'd killed a man for hire. Funny, he couldn't remember the guy's name even though the incident had played such a monumental role in Decker's life.

It was more than a decade earlier. He'd had been working for an organized crime ring as an enforcer. At the time, Ryan Steele had been his partner. Ryan was the brains and Decker, the brawn.

It still stung that Ryan had switched sides and gone to work for the cops.

For years, he'd had help. First, the old lady who lived in Mexico. She was dead—he'd had no choice but to kill her, to keep her from revealing him to the police. Then, there was a hacker named Seraphim, who'd given him money, cars and information. Now, the hacker was in jail. In the end, Seraphim wasn't as smart as he'd thought.

Decker had been on his own before, but never like this. Now, he was stuck in the middle of nowhere. He had food and water—stolen from the campers—but his supplies were dwindling. He needed a car and some cash. And right now, stealing from the search party was the only way he'd get either.

As he stared into the darkness, determination, like a knife's edge, slid along his spine. Hell, he was the descendant of the most famous serial killer of all time. He had the blood of Jack the Ripper in his veins, and he was becoming famous in his own right, as well. But it was more than his family tree that made Decker special.

Because in the end, he was smarter than Ryan. He was meaner, more resourceful, and agile than all of them. He would survive. No matter how many people he had to kill for him to get away.

Hannah and Gypsum offered to take the first watch. With her hot flashes, insomnia, and the shock of finding Slade's body, there was no way she could have fallen asleep. Besides, everyone on the team seemed wiped out and they needed their rest.

And then, there was the fact that she wanted to avoid Bruce and all the emotions she wanted to ignore.

The sun had finally set. Without the brutal heat, the night held a chill. It was mid-May, so a little bit of cold was to be expected—even in Texas. She turned her gaze upward and the stars spread out like diamonds scattered across a carpet of black velvet. She stared into the darkness, as her vision turned fuzzy at the edges. Her shoulders were sore, and her head ached. After standing guard, Hannah was more than tired. She was exhausted. Today had been a long day and with the extra hours of guard duty, she hoped that she was tired enough to rest.

She glanced at her watch. It was two minutes to eleven. That meant that Trey should be coming to relieve her any minute.

As if her misery had summoned him from the night, a shadow emerged.

“Hey,” Trey said. “How are you doing?”

“It’s been a hell of a day,” she said. “Did you get some sleep?”

“Yeah, I got some rest,” he said. “I’ll be good for a while. You go back to camp and get some sleep yourself.”

Even though it was dark, she smiled. “Thanks. Wake us if you see or hear anything.”

Trudging through the night, she returned to camp. There was a fire burning in a pit. Bruce sat on the ground and stared into the flames. He’d slipped a flannel shirt on over his T-shirt. The firelight danced on the planes of his cheeks and chin, turning his features more rugged than should be allowed. She looked away. She’d been able to avoid him all evening, first by setting up the tent with Ezra and then by tending to Gypsum while she ate. Finally, she had volunteered for the first watch with the hopes that he’d be asleep by the time she got done. But could she go on ignoring him?

She supposed that she could. Especially since her wrist still held the memory of his gentle touch. Rubbing her arm against the leg of her pants, Hannah realized there was a different question she should be asking. Should she keep her distance?

He looked up as she approached. “Hey.”

"Hey, yourself. You should get some sleep. It was a long day and tomorrow will be longer."

"I actually got some shut-eye but woke up because Ezra snores." He chuckled. "Thought it was a grizzly bear."

"I didn't think grizzlies were in this part of the country."

"They aren't, so imagine my surprise."

She laughed.

"Have a seat, unless you find the sound of an airplane engine soothing."

"Ezra's snoring can't be that bad," she said, dropping onto the ground across from where Bruce sat.

"Listen for yourself. You can hear him from here."

The fire cracked and popped. In the distance, an owl hooted. The wind whistled as it blew across the grassland. And beneath it all was another sound. It was like the rumbling thunder. Almost, but not quite…

Tilting her head to the side, she listened harder. Then she looked at Bruce. "Is that him? That can't be him."

He chuckled. "It is and it can."

He really was cute when he smiled. Hannah turned her eyes back to the fire. The flames danced and wove, hypnotic in their movements. Her eyelids drooped. A hand touched her shoulder. She sat up straight, her heart slamming against her ribs.

Bruce knelt at her side. "Whoa. Sorry. I didn't mean to scare you."

"I'm just startled," she said, gasping for air. "That's all."

"I woke Ezra, told him he sounded like an out-of-tune motor. He offered to wedge a bag in next to his side to keep from snoring, or he'll come out here. Your choice. I just wanted you to know that you don't need to sleep sitting up."

Before she could make up her mind, Ezra appeared at the fireside. A sleeping bag was slung over his shoulder. "I'll rest out here," he said, laying the bag out by the fire. "It's probably best that not everyone is in the tent anyway. You two go and get some sleep."

Gypsum was already on her feet and pulling toward the tent. The dog had been on enough search and rescue missions to know that it was time to go to bed.

Most of the time, there weren't *his* and *hers* quarters. So, Hannah slept where she could, when she could. But it was also true that she didn't usually work with someone like Bruce—a man she found both appealing and confusing.

With a sigh, she got to her feet. "G'night, Ezra."

He gave her a wan smile. "Night."

At the tent, Gypsum nosed open the flap. Hannah let go of the leash and crawled in after the dog. A lantern hung on the frame of the tent, filling the space with a warm glow. Her canine companion recognized Hannah's sleeping bag and turned a circle before lying down near the foot. Bruce sat on the end of his sleeping bag and pulled off his boots.

When Hannah and Ezra had set up the tent hours earlier, she'd been the one to lay out the sleeping bags, thus assigning spots. At the time, there were four sleeping bags, all in a row. She'd placed hers next to one wall and Bruce next to the opposite wall—putting two people in between them.

Now, with Ezra by the campfire and Trey standing guard, it was just her and Bruce. Her skin tingled with anticipation and desire. But her touch seemed to burn his skin—and not in a good way.

"Mind zipping up the flap?" Bruce asked. "I don't want any critters to wander in during the night."

"Uh, yeah, sure." She knelt next to the zipper and pulled it closed. Then she lifted her own sleeping bag and turned it upside down before shaking it out. Hannah had yet to find one of those "critters" Bruce mentioned finding while on other operations. But she knew it was better to be safe—because climbing into her sleeping bag only to find that a snake had made itself at home would definitely make her sorry.

"I checked all the bags and the tent floor already," he said. "Everything's clear. We should be safe."

Spreading her sleeping bag back on the ground, Hannah sat. She unlaced her hiking boots and slid them off. "Best feeling of the day," she said, curling and uncurling her toes.

"Ain't that the truth," he said.

He stood and unbuttoned the front of his flannel shirt. As he pulled it off his shoulders, the T-shirt underneath rode up, giving her a view of his toned abs and tanned skin. She shouldn't find his twang cute or his blue eyes alluring or his rock-solid torso appealing. But she did.

Maybe it was fine to look a little, especially since she knew enough not to touch.

Hannah busied herself with arranging her sleeping

bag before unzipping the side. She slid inside the folds and the nylon inner layer slipped over her skin like water. Rolling to her side, she tucked her arm under her head and faced the tent wall.

"You all set?" asked Bruce. "If you are, I'm going to turn off the light."

"All set," she said, not bothering to face him.

He turned off the lantern with a click.

The tent was plunged into darkness. Hannah stared at nothing. Gypsum snuggled closer to her feet and let out a contented sigh. She listened to the dog's rhythmic breathing. Closing her eyes, she tried to focus on her own breath. How had she been exhausted less than an hour earlier and now she couldn't sleep?

Yet she knew the answer to that question.

A serial killer was on the loose. One of their team members was dead. Truly, that was enough worry.

But there was someone else occupying her thoughts, as well.

Bruce.

He was too close. His scent—sweat and musk and the wide Texas sky—hung in the air. Images of his bright blue eyes filled her mind and sent her pulse racing. Her hand started to tingle as it went numb. Stretching out her arm, she flopped onto her back.

"Can't sleep?" Bruce asked.

She looked in his direction. Firelight shone on him from behind, turning him into a shadow. "Can't sleep," she echoed.

"I figured without the snoring that I'd be able to rest. But I just realized that..." he said, his words unraveling.

She should let it go and ignore whatever he'd started to say. Hannah knew that to be true. Why then did she blurt out, "You just realized *what*?"

"No, I can't say it. If I do, you'll think I'm a dinosaur. Or worse yet—a caveman."

She faced him completely and propped her head onto her hand. "Now you have to tell me. Besides, I happen to like dinosaurs."

Gypsum grunted and got to her feet. She wandered into the space between them before dropping with a huff.

"I just don't know what to say or how to make it come out right."

"Go ahead and blurt it out. I won't complain to HR or anything. I promise."

He rolled toward her. His features were completely lost in the gloom and yet she could feel his eyes on her. "It's just I haven't slept next to a woman since my wife..." His words trailed off again. "Even in my own ears that sounds awkward as hell. Forget I said anything. Please."

Hannah knew that forgetting about this conversation was for the best. She wasn't looking for love. And Bruce had been right—everything about this situation was awkward as hell. But her interest was piqued. She rolled onto her back and stared at the roof. Even in the dark, the lantern glinted with the firelight. At least now she knew why he never wore a wedding ring.

"I've been divorced," she said even before she decided to speak. "Twice. I know how it can be when a marriage falls apart. It's hard at first. But if you want to find someone again, you will."

Hannah wasn't sure that she believed her own words. After all, she had tried for love after her first marriage. It had worked out just as badly the second time. In the silence, she wondered if she was the problem.

"It wasn't a divorce," he said, pulling her from her thoughts. "Pamela, that is—was—my wife. Well, she died."

Dammit all. Hannah had stepped in it now. "I am so sorry."

He raised his hand, just a shadowy outline against the firelight. "You don't have to say anything. I appreciate your condolences. But it was a long time ago. I just wanted you to know—that's all."

What was she supposed to say now? "Thanks for your honesty. And, really, I am sorry."

He let out a long breath. "Well, I better try and get some rest. I have the last watch."

"Good night, then."

Gypsum slipped her muzzle under Hannah's hand. As she petted the dog, she tried to categorize all her questions. But mostly she wondered how she was supposed to get any sleep now.

Bruce lay in the dark and listened to Hannah breathing quietly. It had taken some time, but she'd finally drifted to sleep. Yet he had to wonder why he had shared anything about Pamela's death. He rarely mentioned anything personal to anyone—especially someone he'd just met.

But Hannah was different.

She was less like a new acquaintance and more like

an old friend who he hadn't seen in years. He wanted to know everything about her—and to share bits of his life, too. He pulled in a sharp breath and tightened his stomach, waiting for the gut punch that came with guilt over straying too far away from Pamela's memory.

It didn't come.

It was the second time in a single day that it had happened.

What was wrong with him?

He glanced at Hannah. She was sleeping on her side, facing him. Her lips were slightly parted and her lashes rested on her rosy cheeks. Her chest rose and fell with each breath, the fabric of the sleeping bag draped over her hip showing off her womanly curves. He shouldn't be ogling her. But Bruce couldn't look away, even if he tried.

Gypsum rose from the ground and walked to the far side of Hannah. In her sleep, Hannah stirred as the dog stretched out beside her, placing all four paws on Hannah's back. She inched away from Gypsum and closer to Bruce. He could feel her breath on his shoulder, his cheek, his chest. She flopped to her stomach; her arm outstretched. Her fingertips brushed his hand.

His skin warmed where her fingers grazed his palm. Thcrc was nothing mcant by thc touch. It was an accident, nothing more. Yet his mouth went dry. The firelight shone through the thin fabric of the tent's wall and danced across her features, turning her to bronze. God, she really was pretty. He also appreciated her honesty and bravery.

Bruce was out here because he knew the area and

Mercy was his home. Decker had caused too much death and destruction for him to look away. But Hannah was new to town, and still she was doing the right thing. He admired that in a person—forget that she looked like a goddess.

Closing his eyes, Bruce tried to force himself to sleep. But his mind was on overdrive and wouldn't give him any rest. Like always, his thoughts returned to Pamela when she was in her last days—home with hospice after a final treatment in San Antonio. The medication had done nothing to stop or cure the cancer.

She'd been sleeping. He'd been sitting at her bedside, watching her chest rise slowly and then fall. The whole time, he'd prayed that her next breath would not be her last. The room had been filled with the sickly-sweet scent of decay. He'd risen to open the window, but there wasn't the slightest breeze to stir the air.

When he'd sat back down, she was the one watching him. "This is it," she'd said.

He'd known it was true. Her skin was paper-thin, the veins clearly visible. She'd lost all her hair, her brows and lashes, too. There were dark circles around her eyes, making her look more like a skull than he cared to admit.

"Don't say that." He'd reached for her hand. Her fingers so delicate, it was like holding a baby bird. "They're developing new treatments every day. I was looking online and there's a hospital in New York City. They're running tests on a new drug for your type of cancer. It should only be a few more months and they'll start with human trials. We can talk to your doctor about getting you on that list..."

She'd gripped his hand with a strength that surprised him. "I don't have months. I don't have weeks. I don't even know if I have days. This is it for me, and I don't want to waste my time wishing for things that won't happen."

Her words had hollowed him. Gutted. Without her, he was empty, and he knew that he'd collapse from the weight of his grief. "Pamela, I don't know what to do without you. How am I supposed to give Shana advice on her wedding day? Or what do I tell her when she has her first baby?"

She'd closed her eyes and smiled. "You'll think of something, I'm sure."

He remembered thinking, *How am I supposed to go from us and we to* me*?* Alone.

For a long moment, she'd said nothing. He'd thought she'd gone back to sleep. Bending to her, he'd placed his lips on her cheek and whispered, "I will always love you."

"I don't want you to be by yourself. After I'm gone, find someone else. Promise me that—"

Bruce gasped and opened his eyes. He was still in the tent. Still in the wilderness. Still on the hunt for the killer. The words had been so clear, it sounded as if they'd been spoken out loud and not just in his mind. He supposed that memory was a funny thing. Most of the time, his remembrances ended with him swearing his undying love.

But in reality, there had been more.

Next to him, Hannah's fingertips still lay on his open palm. She twitched in her sleep, clutching his fingers.

For the first time in years, he felt as if he were filled again. Whole. Complete.

Bruce exhaled, knowing that Hannah hadn't intended to hold his hand. But it felt right, just the same. This time, when he closed his eyes, there was nothing to see and sleep finally came to claim him.

Chapter 7

Hannah woke slowly, sleep clinging to her like a fog. Like every morning, Gypsum, stretched out and pressed up against her back, had pushed her to the edge of her bed.

No, that wasn't right. Sure, her canine companion was at her side. But she wasn't on a mattress or even in her room. She was in a tent and sleeping in her sleeping bag. But that still didn't explain why her head rested on a man's chest. The scent of him—sweat, musk and sky—clung to her skin and his pulse echoed beneath her cheek. His arm was draped over her shoulder. What the hell?

Sitting up, she rubbed her eyes. Then she recalled her latest mission to find the at-large killer, Decker Newcombe. The light in the tent was soft and gray, surrounding everything in a haze. Bruce McDaniel was asleep at her side. Suddenly she understood everything. Gypsum, like she always did, had pushed on Hannah in the middle of the night. Yet, instead of running out of room on the mattress, she'd ended up in Bruce's arms.

Pulling her hair back, she wound it into a bun before wrapping an elastic band around her tresses. The best thing was to sneak away before Bruce woke up and realized what she had done.

She glanced at him. He watched her with one eye open.

“Morning,” he said, his voice husky with sleep.

Crap. It was too late to sneak away now.

“Good morning,” she said, her voice too loud in the quiet of a new day.

Sliding upright, Bruce rubbed his face with both hands. Overnight, his beard had come in. Now, there was a sprinkling of hair on his cheeks and chin. It looked soft and her fingers itched with the need to touch his face.

“How’d you sleep?” he asked, pinning her in place with his aqua-blue eyes.

Hannah paused a beat. She wasn’t tired, the way she usually was in the morning—thanks to perimenopause. In fact, she was well rested. “I feel pretty good actually.”

Beside her, Gypsum lifted her head and looked at Hannah over her shoulder. The dog thumped her tail on the ground. “Looks like she got a good night’s sleep, too,” she said, running her hands through the canine’s thick fur.

“That’s what hiking in the heat and then all this fresh air will get you,” he said.

“I suppose so.”

Hannah knew better, though. She’d slept so well because she’d spent the night in Bruce’s arms. It wasn’t something she’d set out to do. But even in her sleep, she’d been drawn to him. At her most basic level, she knew he would keep her safe while she was vulnerable. At the same time, he’d told her that his wife had died years earlier. If she had to guess, she'd say that he wasn't over that loss. Even if she wanted a new romance, Hannah didn't want to get her heart broken again. And that meant she needed some distance from Bruce. "Well, I better get Gypsum outside."

"Don't forget to check your shoes before you put them on," he said while unzipping his sleeping bag.

He was right. Even with the flap shut, it was still possible for bugs to make their way into the tent. She reached for her shoes and turned them upside down. Banging the sides together, she shook them, knocking out anything that might have crawled inside. Thankfully, her hiking boots were empty.

As she slipped them on and tightened the laces, Gypsum pawed at the tent's flap. Hannah clipped the leash on the dog's harness and unzipped the tent. She crab-walked outside and stood tall. Her spine popped as her joints realigned.

Trey was sleeping near the embers of the dying fire and Ezra was standing on a rock formation several yards from the camp. Raising a hand in greeting, he said, "Morning. Hope you slept well."

Hannah waved back. "I did. Thanks. How long have you been standing guard?"

After glancing at his watch, he said, "Since one this morning. So, four hours."

Why hadn't he woken Bruce? After all, he was supposed to take the final watch of the night. Before she could say anything, Ezra answered her unasked question. "I wasn't tired at all. It seemed a shame to wake you both. So I just stayed up."

Obviously, Ezra had noted that she and Bruce were sleeping alone in the tent. Was he just being considerate? Or had he thought that something else was going on? Or, worst of all—had he actually peeked into the tent and seen Hannah sleeping in Bruce's arms? Was that when he'd decided to leave them alone?

She wasn't going to apologize for being a woman with needs—both sexual and physical. Since nothing had happened, she hated for her new colleagues to get the wrong idea. All the same, she'd been around long enough to know that trying to correct a story would cause more problems than it solved. She tilted her chin to the side of the camp. "I'm going to walk Gypsum. I'll be back in a minute."

"Make that a second," said Trey. He unzipped his sleeping bag and scrambled to his feet. "I want to find Slade's gun now that there's enough light for us to see."

Walking just outside the perimeter, she found a spot and gave the command. "Business." The dog was so well trained that she knew what to do.

Within moments, both Hannah and Gypsum returned to camp. Bruce was boiling water over the propane stove. He wore yesterday's flannel shirt and his cowboy hat. He looked up as she approached. "Coffee will be ready in a minute."

"I thought that Trey wanted to leave now," she said, poking at the charcoals of the fire with a stick. A spark popped up and she shoved a handful of grass near the glowing coals. Immediately, the kindling began to smoke and smolder.

"Trust me," said Bruce. "We'll all do better with full bellies and a little caffeine."

She prepared a dish of kibble for Gypsum and set it on the ground. As the dog ate, Hannah fed logs into the fire.

"Water's ready to make coffee," said Bruce, pouring boiling water into a cup. "And there's breakfast food in the box."

The air-dropped rations was just a cardboard container filled with MREs, along with granola bars, applesauce packets and dehydrated eggs. None of the food was what she'd considered tasty. Still, it was palatable enough and would give them energy for a full day in the desert.

Even though Trey was eager to find Slade's missing gun, he must've seen the sense in eating while he could. He opened a box of granola bars and took two packets for himself. He handed the box to Hannah. "Here you go."

She took two packets and passed them on to Ezra. Then she filled her own cup with hot water and a spoonful of instant coffee. The water turned murky before the nutty aroma of coffee drifted up in a cloud of steam.

After opening one of her granola bars, she took a bite. The crunchy combination of nuts and oats were both sweet and had a hint of spicy cinnamon. For a few minutes, everyone ate and drank in silence. The first rays of sun crept over the eastern horizon as Hannah drank the last of her coffee. She refilled her water bladders and stowed them, along with the collapsible dog dish, into her bag. Then she brushed her teeth and applied sunscreen.

Everyone on the team was wearing yesterday's clothes. Hannah had two more outfits packed in her bag, though she didn't plan to change for forty-eight hours. But, she noticed, Trey's forearms were bright red. Holding out her sunscreen, she offered, "Anyone need this?"

"Yeah," said Trey. "Thanks. Got a little too much sun yesterday."

"You got anything more than a T-shirt to wear?" Bruce asked. "No offense, but sunscreen will only do so much against a burn like that."

Trey removed a white, long-sleeved tee from his bag. "This is all I got," he said. "But it's not exactly camouflage."

"Better than nothing," said Ezra.

Trey sighed and peeled off his T-shirt. "I guess you're right," he said as he donned the long-sleeved shirt. "I think we should stick with the plan we made yesterday. Ezra and I will look for Slade's gun. Bruce and Hannah find a spot with cellular coverage and call Texas Law."

"I still think it's solid, man," said Ezra.

"So do I," Bruce confirmed. "Let me show you where you need to go." He unfolded a topographical map and gave directions back to the canyon. After folding the map and handing it to Trey, Bruce said to Hannah, "You ready?"

"As I'll ever be," said Hannah. And still, she was reluctant to be with Bruce. It meant that they would be together—but alone.

As she hefted her pack onto her back, Hannah knew what she feared the most. Bruce was still in love with his late wife and would never love anyone else. It meant that she was falling for the wrong guy yet again.

* * *

Bruce knew that the closest place to get cell coverage was two miles from where they'd made camp. He pointed toward Ghost Horse Point. The tower of red and brown rocks was stark against the blue sky. "Hannah and I are headed that way," he said to Trey and Ezra. "We aren't going all the way to the Point, but there are a series of hills where we might get some kind of coverage."

"How long will it take, do you think?" asked Trey.

Bruce exhaled. The feeling of Hannah's hand was still imprinted on his chest. "It'll be a ninety-minute round trip, if we're lucky. If we don't find coverage within two hours, we'll head back. So maybe as long as four hours."

"Be back here in three hours," said Trey. "If you haven't found coverage, we'll pack up the camp and return to the vehicle. We can't count this mission as a loss. We know Decker is close. But we're down by one man and we can't leave Slade's body under a bunch of rocks for long. He deserves better."

"That brings up something else," said Ezra. "We're still looking for Decker. Everybody needs to stay sharp."

Bruce had his shotgun. He was ready.

"Let's go," said Hannah. "That way we can all do what we need to do and get back to camp."

Bruce nodded to Trey and Ezra. "Good luck, guys."

"Same to you," said Ezra.

Hannah smiled. "Thanks."

Then the team of four broke into groups of two. They headed in different directions. Bruce and Hannah walked for several minutes without speaking. Once again, he didn't like the silence. He wanted to know more about Hannah. To tell her about himself.

But what was he supposed to say?

Hey, Hannah. In your sleep you reached for my hand. It was nice. It was the first time since becoming a widower that I felt connected to another person.

It didn't matter that every word would be the truth. It was too honest.

He kept walking. Hannah and Gypsum were a few yards ahead of him. It gave Bruce the perfect view of her rear, hips and thighs. She filled out her khaki hiking pants with all the right curves, and he liked the view.

When she stopped, he kept going for a stride or two, more fixated on her butt than what she was doing.

"I figure we can use a break," said Hannah as she loosened the shoulder straps of her bag and let it slip to the ground. She rolled her neck a few times before touching her toes. Still bent over, she removed sunscreen from her bag. Hannah applied cream to her hands, wrists and face. Holding out the tube, she asked, "Want some?"

"Sure." He held out his open palm. Hannah squeezed a line of white balm into his hand. As Bruce rubbed sunscreen onto the bridge of his nose, he said, "We might be able to get a signal from here. Check your phone and see if you have any coverage."

She pulled her phone from her bag as Gypsum plopped onto the dirt and panted. Hannah turned on the device and shook her head. "Nothing."

"Hopefully, we're getting close." Bruce pointed to a nearby knoll. "If we climb that hill, we should be able to get enough of a signal to place a call."

She shoved her phone back into her bag and pulled out a plastic bottle filled with water. She took a long drink, her throat working as she swallowed. There was a dimple at the base of her neck. His imagination took over and in his mind's eye, he placed his lips on that exact spot.

"You want some?" she asked.

Her words dragged him from his fantasy. "Excuse me?"

She held out her bottle to him. "Do you want a sip of water?"

He reached for the bottle. The need to touch her was as natural as the pull of the waves during a hunter's moon. He lifted the bottle to his lips and drank a long swallow. By the time he handed her back the bottle, she had removed a dish for Gypsum. She dumped the rest of the bottle into the bowl, and they waited as the dog drank, as well. "It's gonna be a hot one again today," he said. "You go first. I don't want to tire out the dog. Besides, there might be clues as to Decker's whereabouts."

"It's nice of you to worry about Gypsum." After stowing the empty water bottle in her backpack, she pulled out a baseball cap. She placed the hat on her head and pulled her bun through the opening at the back.

With a click of her tongue, she roused Gypsum. Then she and the dog started to climb the hill.

It took them only a few minutes to make it to the top of the rise. From there, Bruce could see for miles in each direction. The tent where they'd slept the night before was a red speck on the horizon. The canyon, where Trey and Ezra had gone, rose out of the barren ground. Scrawny oaks dotted the brown landscape.

Being this far up left them exposed. If Decker was out there, watching and waiting, he would be able to see them. Bruce scanned the horizon for movement. In the distance, a coyote scampered out from behind a large boulder. The wild canine had its nose to the ground, having caught the scent of something. It was gone as quickly as it came. In the sky, a hawk rode the waves of heat that were already forming troughs in the air.

On the summit, Hannah took her phone out of her backpack. She'd turned off the power overnight to save her charge. It had worked. She still had fifty percent battery life. "I have one bar," she said with a smile. "It should be enough to make a call."

"Thank God."

Hannah entered the number for Texas Law. Even with the phone pressed to her ear, he could hear the three tones and a recorded message.

Your call did not go through.

"Dammit," she cursed. "There are no more bars. I thought there was supposed to be coverage all over the state."

"There's coverage everywhere there are people. This is more like no-man's-land." He paused a moment and thought through their next steps. "The next hill over is higher up." Even from their position, he could tell that the face was steeper and more rocks littered the incline. Still, Hannah was strong and fit—maybe even in better shape than he was. They would both be able to handle the hike. "We're more likely to get a signal there."

She sighed, her shoulders sagging. He hated to see her disappointed.

"It'll be okay," he said, placing his hand on her shoulder. Her muscles were firm, and her skin was soft. She was everything he wanted in a woman. But was he ready to move on from his former spouse?

It occurred to Bruce that he'd never thought about Pamela as his former spouse before. In his mind, she'd always been his wife.

Bruce let his hand slip away. He balled his fingers into a fist, fighting the urge to touch Hannah again. "It's not that much farther of a walk. We've got plenty of water, and I'll bet that we get a strong signal over there."

"It's not that," she said. "It's what you said about this search somehow being cursed." She shook her head. "I don't believe in that kind of thing, but it does seem like a lot of bad luck."

"Well, it's time that we change our fortune." He nodded to the other hill. "By climbing up there and making that call."

"The thing that bothers me the most is that we're out here for a reason," said Hannah. A gust of wind blew, whipping away her words. "We're here to find a killer. I can't help but wonder if we're chasing Decker—or if he's coming after us."

Chapter 8

Decker Newcombe needed only one thing. A vehicle so he could escape this godforsaken place. His best chance for getting one was to steal it from the people who had been sent into the desert to catch or kill Decker himself. It left him stalking those who were hunting him.

He needed to do more than watch from afar, but the search dog added a complication. The canine knew his scent and would warn everyone if he got too close. That's why he'd chosen to follow the two men out of the camp. It was a calculated move, to be sure. Especially since the dudes looked to be younger and better armed than the other man and the woman with the dog.

After watching the men for several minutes, he knew they were headed back to the place where he'd shoved the guy off a cliff. He also figured that they were looking for the dead guy's gun. It was the same firearm Decker now carried in his backpack.

Having spent weeks alone, he knew all the places to hide, to watch, and to wait. He also knew how to come around the canyon from the opposite side. It might take some time, but Decker could be patient when he needed to be. He'd been waiting a long time to take his revenge on Ryan Steele, his former friend and partner in crime. Now the pieces were finally falling into place. As soon as he grabbed this car, he'd be one step closer to that goal to be the most famous serial killer of all time.

His ties to Jack the Ripper had already given him a measure of notoriety. But he wanted more. He'd been born to kill. To terrorize. Just his name would send a shiver down spines. In years to come, Decker wanted to live on imaginations as the monster that lurked in the darkness.

Ezra followed Trey as they walked in silence to where Slade had fallen from the cliff. He understood his colleague's desire to find the lost firearm. In fact, he shared it. But he also thought there were more important things to worry about, like alerting the rest of the Texas Law team that one of their own was dead. Hannah and Bruce were taking care of that task. But Ezra wasn't happy that they'd broken into two groups. The search party should always stick together.

Even a man as devious as Decker Newcombe would have a hard time taking down a group of four well-trained individuals—especially since they had a dog to give them plenty of warning. "I don't like that we split up," he said at last. "Look what happened to Slade when he took off on his own."

Trey glanced at Ezra. "Nobody has gone solo. Besides, we have to get the gun and make a call. There's not enough time to do both separately."

He couldn't argue with that logic. "It doesn't mean I like the situation."

"I don't like it, either," said Trey. "But it can't be helped."

The mouth of the canyon opened like a yawn. The rock walls blocked out the rays of the rising sun and still held some of the night's chill. It took them only minutes to find the place where Slade had fallen. The ground was still black with his dried blood. The scuff marks were still visible from where he'd climbed.

Ezra's throat tightened. "Hell of a thing," he said. "Here one minute. Gone the next."

Trey let out a long breath and turned in a slow circle. There was nothing but sandy ground and rocky walls as far as the eye could see. "Obviously, the Glock's not down here."

Ezra looked up, his gaze scaling the canyon wall. It didn't matter that he was still on the ground, the height left him dizzy. "I can't see anything from here. But maybe the gun landed on one of the ledges. Or it could be at the top, if Slade made it that far." He paused. "Or maybe the killer got to him up there."

"Let's go up there and see what we can find."

"You want to climb that thing? Uh-uh. No way."

Trey raised a single eyebrow. "You afraid of heights or something?"

"I'm not afraid of the height," Ezra said, although his words were a lie. "It's the falling that bothers me."

"You wait here," said Trey, strapping his rifle to his back. "I'm going to climb up there and see what I can find."

"You sure that's safe?"

"I was trained on this in the army," said Trey. "And I go rock climbing for fun."

Ezra tamped down the urge to shiver. "That doesn't sound like much fun to me."

"I'll be back in a minute."

Trey raised himself onto a ledge that was about six feet from the ground. He reached above his head and found a set of handholds. Ezra had to admit his teammate looked confident, like he knew what he was doing. And still, he could feel his pulse climb with each foot that Trey gained. Looking away, he began to pace. He glanced back at his fellow operative. Trey was halfway to the rim. "Find anything?" He raised his voice to be heard at a distance.

"Not yet. I'll finish the climb and see if the gun is up top."

"I'll still be down here. Waiting. Sweating," he said, trying to make a joke about his fear.

But there was more to be concerned about than Trey falling, which was bad enough. Ezra had split up with his partner once again. It left them both vulnerable. Reaching for the holster at his hip, he unfastened the thumb break and removed his Walther PDP. It was a reliable service weapon, and the same kind he'd carried while working for the Miami PD.

When he looked up next, Trey had reached the top of the canyon. The rising sun caught him from behind, making him little more than a silhouette that shouted, "I still don't see anything. But I'll look around for a minute."

"Be careful," Ezra called out.

Trey backed away from the edge, disappearing from view. Ezra let out a long breath and that's when he felt it. Cold metal boring into the base of his skull. His blood turned icy in his veins.

Someone had him at gunpoint.

No, not just a random person. It was Decker Newcombe.

The fact that Ezra had been right about Decker killing Slade and then stealing his gun brought him no joy.

"Do exactly as I say," the killer whispered. His stale breath washed over Ezra's cheek. "And you won't get hurt."

He still held his own firearm. But would Ezra be quick enough to fire on Decker before getting shot? Could he call out for Trey before taking a bullet to the head? He knew the answer to each question was no. "I'm listening."

"First, you're going to hand me your gun. Hook one finger around the trigger guard and pass it back nice and slow."

Ezra did as he was told. Decker jerked the gun out of his hand.

Without a gun, Ezra had only two weapons. His wits and time. Trey would only search the plateau for so long before looking over the edge. From there, picking off Decker would be an easy shot. All Ezra needed to do was to keep the killer calm. "What do you want?"

"Keys to your vehicle." Decker pressed the barrel of the gun harder into Ezra's skull.

"I don't have them," he said, being honest. Trey had the keys to SUV.

"Where are they?"

In an instant, he knew what would happen if he told him the truth. Decker would keep Ezra as a hostage until Trey reappeared. The minute Decker had the keys, he'd shoot Ezra in the back of the head.

No. He couldn't tell the truth. He said, "They're back at the camp in a box with a combination lock."

There was no such box at the camp, and he was taking a risk in lying to Decker. After all, the killer might have already looked through their belongings and know.

"What's the combination?"

"No way." The only way to survive was to be useful. Besides, the walk would give Trey time to realize something was wrong. Or if Ezra was really lucky, Hannah and Bruce would already be back at the camp. "I'll take you there and open it for you."

Decker shoved the gun into his head. The barrel left a bruise on his scalp. "What's the goddamn combination?"

"If I tell you now, you'll kill me. It'll suck for you. Trey will hear the blast." Ezra turned his gaze to the cliff, hoping to catch sight of his Trey. The ridgeline was empty. "Then, my buddy up there will shoot you himself."

For a moment, Decker stayed silent. He must've understood the truth in what had been said because the pressure on the gun increased. Shoving Ezra forward with the barrel, the killer said, "Walk. Fast."

Ezra dragged his foot through the sandy soil, leaving a gouge in the ground. It wasn't much. Hopefully, it was enough of a clue for Trey to know that something was really wrong.

Using the gun, the killer drove Ezra forward. "Who do you work for?"

"Texas Law."

"You work for Ryan Steele?"

Ezra knew the history between the two men. How they'd been friends at one time, but Ryan had teamed up with the cops to help find and stop the killer. It was dangerous to admit an allegiance to someone who Decker must loathe. "He's a colleague."

"Never trust him," said Decker. "He's a snake. Worse than a snake."

For a single heartbeat, he was buoyed by hope. Maybe the killer really did want the keys to the vehicle, and once he got what he wanted, then he'd let Ezra go. But it was only wishful thinking.

By the time the camp came into view, he still didn't have a plan. He listened, hoping that Gypsum would give a warning bark. The only sounds were the crunching of their footfalls on the ground and the cry of a lone hawk as it circled in the sky.

If Ezra wanted to stay alive, he had to save his own life.

Near the firepit, Decker shoved him forward by the shoulder. He asked, "Where's the lockbox with the keys?"

"Over there." He pointed to the cooler that sat on the ground. "Inside that."

Ezra glanced over his shoulder. It was the first time he'd seen the killer up close and personal. Long hair hung over his shoulders. His lips were cracked. His nose was red, and his skin flaked with sunburn. A long-sleeved shirt hung off his shoulders. Pants ballooned around his legs and were held on to his thin waist with a belt that was cinched tight.

It seemed like weeks earlier Ezra had processed the site of the massacre, not less than a day. There, he'd noted that Decker had stolen the personal belongings from those he'd killed. Obviously, the clothes the killer now wore belonged to one of the men who'd been slaughtered. To Ezra, it seemed like a final disrespect, and filled him with cold determination.

"Go ahead," said Decker, twitching the barrel of the gun. "Get the keys. And remember, I'm watching. You do anything stupid, and I'll shoot you in the back."

He walked slowly to the cooler and knelt on the ground. Holding up one hand, he said, "I'm going to open it now."

"Go ahead," said Decker. "Nice and slow, so I can see what you're doing."

Ezra's other hand was tucked in next to his leg. He scooped up a handful of dirt. Lifting the lid, he leaned forward. As he peered into the cooler, he glanced over his shoulder. Like he'd hoped, the killer had come closer. Without thought and without warning, Ezra threw the dirt into Decker's face.

Decker rubbed his eyes with the back of his hand. "Bastard," he snarled.

Leaping to his feet, Ezra grabbed the gun with both hands and wrenched the firearm from the killer's grasp. He flipped the gun around, holding it by the grip. Before he could aim or fire, the killer lunged forward. Ezra only saw the flash of metal in the morning light before a cold steel blade slid under his chin. Hot blood spurted from the hole in his neck. Pain exploded, like a bomb went off in his body. His legs went numb, and he collapsed to the ground. His vision wavered and then he went blind. He never did see the knife.

Chapter 9

Gypsum pulled on the leash, determined to get to the top of the hill. As Hannah trudged behind, she wished that she had the canine's ability to be single-minded.

This morning, she had a single task—to find a spot with cell coverage. She should focus on that, but she couldn't. Somewhere, out in the hills, was a killer. Decker could be anywhere. Hell, in her mind, he was behind every tree, rock and bush.

She had to focus. To be vigilant. Being distracted by fear was the best way for Hannah to get hurt. And out here, even a simple injury could be deadly.

She walked on, watching. Waiting. Listening. Bruce's breathing was a whisper against her neck. She shook her head, ridding her mind of thoughts of Bruce. It didn't matter that sleeping next to him had been nice. He was still in love with his late wife. He hadn't told her about his feelings. Then again, he didn't need to say a word. She could tell.

Maybe it was all for the best. After all, she wasn't looking for a forever kind of love. Hell, she didn't believe those kinds of romances existed.

That's when Gypsum stopped, mid-stride. Hannah

tripped over the dog's haunches, windmilling her arms to stay upright. With a whine, the canine turned and pulled her toward the base of the hill. The force from the leash jerked her backward.

For a split second, gravity took over and dragged Hannah down. Then Bruce gripped her waist, holding her up from behind. Her back was pressed into his chest. His muscles were strong. His legs were long. His scent filled her lungs.

Her pulse started to race, and her mouth went dry. Having him this close, with his arms around her, was too much. She should step away from his embrace. The thing was, she didn't want to.

"Are you okay?" he asked, whispering the words in her ear.

She was so much more than simply okay. But couldn't say that—not to a man who was still grieving his wife. Still, she turned to face him. He pulled her closer and watched her with those turquoise eyes of his. Looking at him was like diving into the ocean. The thing was, she didn't want to come up for air. He held her tighter, pressing her breasts into the hard planes of his chest. He bent toward her, placing his lips on hers. He kissed her. Softly. Gently. Just the faintest pressure.

Yet, Hannah wanted more. She wanted to taste Bruce. To feel his hands on her. To touch him in return.

And that's when her dog let out a loud bark. The canine heaved and the leash slipped from her hand. The fibers rubbed her palm raw. But she didn't care about the pain.

Gypsum ran down the hill.

Her dog had never taken off like that. Hannah's heart thrummed against her ribs.

"Stop!" she called out. "Heel. Sit."

None of the commands registered. Gypsum continued to run. It didn't matter how nice Bruce's arms felt or that she wanted to kiss him again. Her dog wasn't just a pet. She was her partner. Her companion. Her family.

Hannah sprinted after the canine. "Stop. Sit. Come back."

Gypsum glanced over her shoulder but kept going. Hannah continued running, despite the pull in her side or the fire that filled her lungs with each breath. As Gypsum darted ahead, a cold knot of dread clogged Hannah's throat. What if she never caught the dog? What would happen if her companion disappeared into the desert?

Bruce ran at her side. The shotgun was strapped to his back, the stock slapping his legs with each long stride. He passed her and lunged down to scoop up the leash. He slowed to a jog. Hannah continued running, until she caught up.

Kneeling next to her dog, she pulled Gypsum into an embrace. "What's gotten into you?"

She was rewarded with a lick to the cheek. Then the Lab tried to pull away again.

Standing, Hannah inhaled a deep breath. "What is it, girl? What's gotten you so spooked?"

Looking back at Hannah, the dog whined.

"Whatever it is," said Bruce, "she thinks it's important."

He was right. Wrapping the leash around her wrist

once and once again, she said, "Let's see where she takes us."

In a matter of minutes, their red tent was visible at a distance.

"You think there's something wrong at the campsite?" she asked.

"It's hard to tell from here." Bruce reached for his shotgun, holding the stock with one hand and the barrel with the other.

Gypsum stood at her side, pressing her body weight into Hannah's leg. The dog licked the air, a sure sign that she was anxious. Stroking the top of the canine's head, she asked again, "What is it, girl?"

The air was heavy and pressed Hannah down. She scanned the horizon. The topography looked the same as it had before. Rocks. Dirt. Emaciated trees. Sun. Sky. A hawk circling overhead, its cry piercing the silence.

The hair at Gypsum's nape stood on end and the dog gave a low growl. Without question, there was something—or someone—in the camp. Had Decker found them?

Bruce took a step forward and then another. Hannah followed. Her steps crunching on the gravel sounded like a thunderclap. Her heart hammered, sending her pulse racing. Sweat gathered at her hairline and snaked down her back.

A line of bushes separated them from the camp. Through the spindly branches, she could see the tent. The cooler. The firepit.

"Nothing looks out of the ordinary."

Bruce stepped from behind the line of bushes. Raising one hand, he motioned for Hannah to come forward. There, propped against a rock, was Ezra. His legs were stretched out, his arms folded across his chest. A ball cap was pulled low over his eyes. Tension slipped from her shoulders as she exhaled.

"I didn't realize that he came back and took a nap," she said, her words breaking free with the bubble of a laugh. "He took a double watch last night. I guess he was tired."

That's when she noticed things that she hadn't before. The camp was silent—not filled with Ezra's snores or even his breathing. He was too still. Too quiet. As they moved closer, she noticed soil had been piled in one spot. Bruce dug into the mound with the toe of his boot. The ground was black.

"Blood."

She dropped down on the ground next to Ezra, Gypsum trailing behind her. She lifted the operative's ball cap. There was a large gash at the base of his throat. His dark shirt was covered in blood. His skin was the color of used paste. His lips were blue. Without question, he was dead. Still, she lifted his wrist. His flesh was warm but there was no pulse. She felt his other wrist. There was nothing.

Meeting Bruce's eyes, she shook her head. "He's gone." Then she touched the gore on his neck. The blood was still wet. Hannah got to her feet and wiped her hands on the seat of her pants. "But he hasn't been dead long."

"Where's Trey?" asked Bruce. "What happened out here?"

As he searched Ezra's body, no doubt seeking the

weapon that was likely no longer there, he added, "And where in the hell is Decker Newcombe right now?"

The manhunt had gone from bad to worse in a matter of seconds. Bruce wasn't sure which catastrophe needed his attention first.

"If Ezra hasn't been dead for long..." Bruce looked down at the body of his murdered comrade. Anger and regret, dual vices, wrapped around his chest and made it hard to breathe. He glanced at Hannah and continued. "Then Decker Newcombe is still close by."

"If Ezra was murdered, then Slade's death wasn't an accident, either."

Before Bruce could say anything, Gypsum gave a single bark. It was like the crack of a whip in the quiet morning.

Lifting the shotgun up to his shoulder, Bruce looked through the scope. He scanned the desert, looking for whatever the dog had sensed. Less than one hundred yards away, he could see a flash of white against the sunbaked earth. It was gone as suddenly as it appeared. His pulse raced, echoing in his skull.

He saw it again. A blur against the brown rocks.

This time, he was certain. It was the sleeve of a shirt. There'd been a glint of metal—like the sun reflecting off the barrel of a gun. Whoever was coming into the camp was running fast, and what's more, they were armed.

Staring down the barrel, Bruce tried to gauge where the person would be next.

"Don't." Hannah placed her hand on his arm. Her touch sizzled into his skin. "It's not Decker."

He'd seen Ezra's body. He'd buried too many friends. He wasn't about to let the killer get away again. Or worse yet, let Decker hurt Hannah. He shifted his aim, ready to fire.

"Don't," she said again. Her voice held a flinty edge. "Look at Gypsum."

The dog was tracking the runner, as well. Yet her tongue hung from the side of her mouth. Her tail was a wagging blur. She barked again. This time, he heard the happy tone.

Bruce moved his finger back to the trigger guard and watched through his scope. A man emerged from behind an outcropping of rocks. She was right, it wasn't Decker. It was Trey. Bruce's stomach clenched like a fist. He'd almost fired on his colleague. With a swallow, he lowered his firearm.

Hannah started to call out but then stopped herself.

The other man slowed his sprint to a jog. "We have a problem." Without waiting for a response, he went on. "I climbed up to where Slade fell. There are two sets of footprints and scuff marks at the top. I think he made it all the way up but was pushed. There was no sign of his gun, either. Then, when I got to the bottom, Ezra was gone. I ran back as fast as I could…" His words trailed off as his gaze landed on the feet of his fellow operative. "Is that him?" he asked. "Is he…?"

"Ezra's dead," said Bruce, hating the truth but refusing to say anything else. "Looks like he was stabbed in the throat."

"Did you get ahold of Texas Law?" Trey asked.

"We never did find a signal," Bruce said. "The dog started acting anxious and led us back here."

"My guess is that she caught the scent of Decker—or of the killing—and brought us back to help," said Hannah.

"What do we do now?" After a pause, Trey answered his own question. "We have to hike back to the vehicle now. We'll make a call as soon as we get a signal. But we've lost two men already and need backup." He patted down Ezra's body. "It looks like Decker took his gun, as well."

Bruce didn't like that Decker was armed and clearly dangerous. "Let's gather up what we can carry—water, food, the tent."

"What about Ezra?" Hannah asked. "We can't leave him out here. You saw what happened to the other men Decker killed."

Bruce wanted to get started as soon as possible. Even though they were well stocked with water, it would be difficult to hike during the hottest part of the day. It meant they only had a few hours before they needed shade and would have to wait for the sun to go down. But he also knew that she was right. "We'll bury him like we did Slade. When the helicopter comes back to pick up one body, they can get them both."

"Do we have another tarp?" Hannah asked.

Trey said, "I don't remember seeing a second one. But I can check."

The goods that had been air-dropped were stacked in a neat pile near the cooler that held the water and the box filled with MREs.

Bruce and Hannah waited as Trey searched through the gear. He liked being at her side. He'd liked the way she felt in his arms. He also liked the way her lips felt pressed against his. True, it wasn't much of a kiss. But it left him wanting more.

Letting out a long breath, he cleared his thoughts of Hannah. It was obvious that Decker was picking them off—one by one. Despite the sun and the heat, he shivered.

"Dammit all," Trey cursed.

"What's the matter now?" Hannah asked, stepping toward the stack of gear.

Bruce followed her, sticking to her like a shadow. "If we don't have a second tarp, we can bury him without it. Or we can use one of the sleeping bags."

"Decker took all of our food." Trey stood up and scanned the horizon. "He took one of the rucksacks and loaded it with all of our water, too."

They wouldn't survive for long without water—especially if they had hours of walking ahead of them. At least they'd all stocked up with provisions before leaving in the morning. "If we conserve our supplies, we should be able to get back to the vehicle." Bruce moved to Ezra's body and opened his backpack. Bingo.

He removed three liters of water and four granola bars. It wasn't much, but the extra supplies might be the difference between life and death.

The group spent the next hour collecting enough rocks to cover Ezra's body. Once again, Bruce was asked to say a few words at the temporary grave site. But there wasn't much he could say, and they all felt the weight of time closing in on them. After a quick prayer, they had to get back to business.

Bruce tucked all of Ezra's water and food into his own backpack. Trey dismantled the tent and stowed it in his bag, as well. "I'm leaving the sleeping bags," he said. "They aren't heavy, but we don't need the bulk. The tent will give us some protection from the sun when it gets really hot."

It was exactly what Bruce would've done, and he appreciated that Trey knew his stuff.

"Ready?" Hannah asked.

"Before we go." Trey removed a black handgun from a holster at his hip. "Did you bring your own firearm?"

Hannah opened her pack and removed a small handgun. "I've got this."

Trey said, "Keep it out and with you at all times. If you see Decker, shoot him."

She tucked it into the webbing on the side of her backpack. "Got it."

They left the camp behind. Bruce was in the lead. His shotgun was out, loaded, and ready to use. He glanced over his shoulder. Hannah and her dog were at his back. Trey was at the end of the line.

The easiest way to get to the vehicle would be by taking a direct path through the canyons. But he wanted to give them as much cover as possible. It meant that he had to use the sparse vegetation and rock formations when he could.

They approached a copse of trees. Bruce knelt and patted the air, a universal signal for everyone to take a knee. "We have to assume that Decker is watching us every second and waiting for a chance to kill us," he whispered. Pointing as he spoke, he continued. "I'm going to run from here to that boulder over there. Trey, you give me cover if any bullets start flying. Once I'm set, Hannah, you and Gypsum come next. Then I'll watch as Trey makes his way. Sound good?"

"Your strategy is good," said Trey. "I like it. But let me go first."

Bruce squeezed Trey's shoulder. "Good luck."

The younger man took off like he'd been launched from a cannon. The operative sprinted the hundred feet in mere seconds. Small puffs of dirt kicked up by his heels hung in the air as he skidded behind the boulder. "Made it," he called out.

"Decker didn't shoot," said Hannah. "He might not even be watching us."

"If we're lucky, he stole all our food and headed into the canyons. But so far, the only luck we've had has been the bad kind." Bruce shook his head. "It could be that he was watching and not ready to shoot when Trey came out. Or maybe he doesn't have a clean shot."

Her eyes went wide and her skin paled.

Dammit, he shouldn't have been so honest.

"You'll be fine. Don't run in a straight line." He held his hand up and cut through the air, creating a serpentine pattern. "Zigzag."

"You want me to zigzag? Will that keep me from getting shot?" Her eyes were wide and filled with fear.

He had to do something more. Trying again, he said, "I'm at your back and Trey is at your front. If we get a hint that Decker is around, we're ready to shoot. He won't have enough time to fire at you because he'll be dodging bullets."

She exhaled and stroked the dog's snout. "You want to go for a run?"

Gypsum's tail thumped on the ground at the word *run.* Hannah rose and stood in a crouch. "Let me know when to go."

"You ready?" Bruce moved to Hannah's side. She was close enough that he could touch her if he wanted. What if it was the last chance he ever got?

"I think so." She drew in a deep breath.

Pursing her lips, she blew out the air.

He shouldn't think about the pucker or the fact that he'd kissed her earlier. But he couldn't help himself. Before Bruce had decided to act, he placed his lips on her cheek. "Good luck."

She glanced at him. For the span of a heartbeat, his gut sank to his shoes. Bruce had made a mistake. He shouldn't have kissed her—not again. Then she grabbed him by the collar and pulled him to her. She placed her mouth on his. The kiss was hungry, fierce, and over as quickly as it began.

After looping the leash around her wrist, she sprinted toward Trey. Bruce rose to his knee and scanned the horizon to her left. Trey was in a similar position and looking for any threats to Hannah's right. Seconds passed like hours. But she made it to the boulder.

Funny how in the days after his wife died, Bruce had wanted to curl up and die himself. But he hadn't, if for no other reason than he hadn't known how to give up. But from that day to this, he also hadn't had an unblemished reason for wanting to live. Oh sure, there was his daughter. Shana. His boss, Sage, and his coworkers at the Double S Ranch.

Finally, he had something—make that *someone*—who'd brought back the color to his life. For the first time in years, he could see the world clearly. And that world included Hannah. He didn't know exactly what the future held for him, but he wanted to find out.

Rising, he stepped out from behind the trees. Maybe Hannah had been right. Maybe Decker wasn't watching them at all. Maybe they'd make it out alive and then Bruce could start to live again. From behind the boulder, she waved and mouthed the words, *You can do this.*

For her, he could accomplish anything.

Focusing on Hannah's face, he started to run.

Chapter 10

Decker lay on his stomach. A tree towered above him, giving him both shade and camouflage. Through the sights of his stolen gun, he watched the guy in the cowboy hat run from behind a group of trees. Placing the crosshairs on the guy's back, he hooked his finger around the trigger.

In his mind's eye, he saw the bullet strike. Pink mist erupted from the man's chest as he tumbled, mid-step, to the dirt. Decker could imagine watching the life as it left the cowboy's eyes.

That power—the one that decided life or death—was what turned Decker from a mere man and into a god.

If he pulled the trigger now, he'd take the cowboy down. But there would be consequences. The younger guy had a semiautomatic rifle. The woman now carried a handgun, as well. The survivors would know where Decker was hiding and the barrage of bullets that would rain down on him would be epic.

This time, he wasn't killing for art. Or fear. Or fame. All of this was for survival. If Decker wanted to escape—and he did want to get out—then he had no choice but to watch and wait.

Certainly, there were times when Jack the Ripper was denied his prey. Like when the killer was interrupted in the courtyard of a public house. Since there were no lights, other than a few torches, his ancestor had blended into the darkness and escaped. He liked that Jack had been a patient man, choosing his time to kill.

Well, if his ancestor could wait, then so could Decker.

Eventually, the trio would think he was gone. That's when they would all become lazy—or at least complacent. It was when they thought he wasn't looking, that he'd get his best chance.

The cowboy slid, just like he was stealing second base at a major league game and disappeared from view behind the large boulder.

Setting down his gun, Decker picked up his binoculars. The group was on the move again. They were keeping low and moving fast. It would be hard to hit any of them and damn near impossible to get all three. Staying under the tree, he waited a minute and then a minute more. When he was positive that they wouldn't spot him, he shoved to his feet and followed.

At the base of the boulder, he found footprints that led to a large bush. From there, the trail led to a grouping of rocks.

Decker walked slowly, keeping his distance. The last thing he wanted was for the damn dog to pick up his scent. As the sun climbed in the sky, the temperature climbed, as well. Sweat collected at his hairline and streamed down his back, drying immediately.

Despite the blistering heat, was the trio going directly to their vehicle? The sour taste of defeat coated his tongue. He wouldn't be able to overtake the entire group. He needed them alone, one at a time. But if they never stopped, he'd never get a chance to separate them.

Following the trail, he wondered why the name of his ancestor, Jack the Ripper, had survived for centuries. Decker had read plenty of books on the murders. During the fall of 1888, Jack had killed five women. Only five!

How could a measly handful of killings make someone so famous? But it had, and Decker's great-grandfather many generations back was a legend. Fame—now, that was the real power. More even than just deciding who lived or died.

Funny thing, Decker remembered a dream he'd had as kid.

He knelt on the cobbled ground. Mist and smoke hung in the air. It was cold like he'd never known before. A lantern stood at his side, casting a sickly yellow glow on a woman's face. She certainly wasn't pretty. There were bruises around her neck and Decker held a knife. He sliced through her soft belly, laying open layers of skin and fat and muscle. He revealed shiny organs that were slick with blood.

Years later, he'd learned of his relation to the Victorian-era killer. And he realized that the images in that long-ago dream were from that time. It was then that he knew the vision from that night had been some kind of shared memory—passed down from father to son, until it reached Decker. That's when he knew he was special, and he was determined to make his mark.

All these setbacks hadn't stopped his desire for infamy. In fact, they'd only made his thirst for celebrity stronger than before.

It was getting late. He'd walked for more than two hours without stopping. His head throbbed and his tongue was thick in his mouth. He needed a rest. Sitting in the shade of a tree, he leaned against the trunk and removed a bottle of water. Unscrewing the cap, he lifted it to his lips and took a long swallow. He could use this time to come up with a plan. Because Decker knew one thing for sure. He was playing a long game—and this was just the first move.

The sun hung at its apex and shone down with a punishing heat. Removing his hat, Bruce wiped his brow. "We can't go much farther," he said. "Not in these temperatures."

"Over there," said Trey. He wore sunglasses that reflected the light. Since Bruce couldn't see his eyes, it was hard to guess where the other man was looking. Then he saw it. A small hill rose from the ground, a group of trees at the top. "We can set up the tent at the base and someone can use the trees for both shade and cover while standing sentry."

It was the perfect place to rest and wait for the sun to go down.

"We can make it," said Hannah before adding, "Not that there's a whole lot of options."

She was right. It took only a few minutes to walk and a few more minutes to set up the tent.

"I'll take the first watch," said Trey. "We'll work in one-hour shifts."

"I can go second," Bruce offered.

"That works for me," said Hannah. She scratched the back of the dog's neck. "And thanks for giving Gypsum extra time to rest. She needs time out of the sun. But I'll stand guard for the third hour."

Hannah turned for the tent. Once she was inside, Bruce said to Trey, "I'll relieve you in an hour. But if you need anything, get me. I don't want anyone getting sick from the heat."

"Hold up a second," said Trey, shoving his hand into one of the several pockets on his pants. He removed the remote starter for the car and held it up. "Take these. Keep them in your backpack. They're safer with you—at least while I'm on watch."

Bruce held out his hand and Trey pressed the black fob into his palm. Wrapping his fingers around the remote starter, he understood the keys were their single lifeline—and most likely what Decker wanted from them. Unzipping the top of his backpack, he stowed the fob in an inside pocket. "Got them."

Trey nodded toward the hill. "I'm going to see if I can place a call up there."

"I hate to be the pessimist, but I don't think you'll catch a signal." He took a water bottle out of his bag. "Good luck, though," he said, tossing the bottle. "Take this."

Trey caught the water and nodded his thanks. Then he climbed the hill and stood at the base of an oak. The leaves were dull from the heat.

Bruce lingered as the Texas Law operative pulled out his phone. After looking at the screen, Trey shook his head and shoved the device back into his pocket. Finally, the other man settled on the ground with his back against a trunk and the rifle across his knees. It wasn't the best camouflage, considering that the white T-shirt was visible. But it was good enough that if Decker tried to sneak up on the camp, the operative would see him before the killer even knew he'd been found.

Bruce made his way to the tent and lifted the flap. The sun caught Hannah, breaking into rays around her face. He'd never seen such a beautiful woman in all his life. The dog lay on her side. Tongue hanging out of her mouth, she panted.

Hannah glanced up as he entered the tent. "Hey."

Bruce sat at her side. "Hey, yourself."

"So, what do you think?"

"About what?"

"Is Decker out there, watching us, even now? Will we get back to the car tonight?" The corner of her mouth rose in a smile. "You know, the usual stuff."

He chuckled, even though her questions had been deadly serious. "As far as making it back to the vehicle tonight..." He exhaled and shook his head. "I really don't think so. Moving from one point of cover to the next is taking longer than I'd like. But I'd rather us be careful than end up dead."

"So, you do think he's out there watching us?"

The whole time, he'd asked himself the same question. Was Decker out there right now? Was he so determined to get keys to a vehicle—like Warner had reported—that he'd risk his own life by following a group of well-armed individuals? Then again, he had killed two of their members already. Besides, Decker needed a car to make his escape. He'd stolen some provisions but those wouldn't last forever.

Well, when he thought about it that way, the killer had no other choice than to steal their SUV. "He's out there," said Bruce, "watching us."

"We can't just hope that he doesn't shoot us in the back," said Hannah. "There has to be something else we can do."

Hiking out and hoping not to get shot was exactly what Bruce had planned. "Do you have any other suggestions?"

Lying back, Hannah leaned on her elbows and stretched out her long legs. "Can't we set up an ambush or something?"

It was an interesting suggestion—and one that just might work. Except… "If we had the entire team, or even one more person, we could leave two people behind to watch for Decker and take him down. The way it is now, it'd have to be one person alone." He shook his head. "It's too much of a risk. The best we can do is to stay vigilant and know that this heat is as much an enemy to him as it is to us."

"I guess," she said before lying on her back.

"Maybe we can just leave the keys and walk away. After all, we will be able to place a call soon. Texas Law will come and get us. If Decker gets the car, he might leave us alone."

He liked the way her mind worked, finding all possible solutions. But he'd seen too much from Decker. "He won't leave us alone."

She inhaled deeply. Her breasts pressed against the fabric of her tank top. Being around Hannah had ignited a fire in Bruce and reminded him of what it was to be a man. He knew now wasn't the time to be transfixed by her beauty and her strength.

Yet he was.

"Will we make it back?" she asked, glancing at him.

Decker was deadly and desperate. It made for a dangerous combination. Still, he knew that she needed some reassurance. Hell, maybe he needed some, as well. Finally, he said, "We'll make it back."

"That was quite a pause," she said. "Are you sure you aren't telling me what I want to hear?"

It was exactly what he'd done. But there was more. "We can't give in to the doubt and the worry. The only thing we can do is focus on success."

She gave him a small smile. "Thanks for the pep talk."

"Anytime. Now, try to rest. We've still got a lot of ground to cover."

Hannah closed her eyes, and Bruce watched her for a moment. It was torture to be this close to her and not touch her. Then again, Bruce shouldn't want something so badly—especially since he couldn't give in to his longing—not when they had to stay vigilant.

He looked up at the tent's ceiling. The sun, a white ball, was visible through the nylon. A slight breeze blew through the open panels, drying the sweat on his forearms and neck. His own words resonated in his mind.

We can't give in to the doubt and the worry. The only thing we can do is focus on success.

How long had it been since he'd focused on the positives in his life? It had all started when he became a widower. In losing his wife, he'd lost his basic desire to be happy. To connect with someone else.

Hannah had changed that for him. Now, he just had to make it out alive and take the chance he'd been given to start over.

He glanced at Hannah. She was on her side, but her eyes were open. The dog picked up its head. Ears cocked, Gypsum gave a low growl.

"Did you hear that?" she asked, her voice a whisper.

"Hear what?" he asked.

"It sounded like someone is walking close by."

A bitter taste coated his tongue as images flashed through his mind. Slade, on the ground, his neck twisted and his body broken. Ezra, his skin gray and his lips blue, a stab wound to his neck.

Bruce would never forgive himself if Decker had snuck up on the camp while he was daydreaming about Hannah. His firearm lay at his side. He picked up the shotgun. "I'll check it out," he said. "Wait here."

Hannah sat up and reached for her backpack. She removed her handgun from the webbing on the bag. "I'm coming with you," she said to Bruce. To the dog, she said, "Stay."

Bruce wanted to keep her safe. But he didn't have time to argue. He stepped out of the tent. Somehow, it was hotter outside. Hannah was at his back.

The moment he stood straight, he knew what Hannah and Gypsum had heard. Trey, at the top of the hill, his long-sleeved white T-shirt blinding in the sun, was walking back to his spot by the tree.

"Everything okay?" Bruce asked him.

"Just seeing if I can get a signal from the other side of the hill." Standing at the top of the rise, Trey used his hand to shield his eyes. "No luck, though. Are you both okay?"

"I heard something," said Hannah, "and got spooked. Must've been you walking around."

"Better to stay frosty than get sloppy," said Trey. "Sorry I bothered you both."

"It's not a bother." Bruce wanted to get back into the tent and be alone with Hannah. But it was a distraction that he couldn't afford. "You want me to switch places with you?"

Trey looked at the watch on his wrist. "I've been out here less than a half hour. You stay out of the sun. I'll get you when it's time to switch."

Bruce gave him a thumbs-up. "I'll let you get back to it, then."

Hannah shook her head before ducking down to climb back into the tent. Gypsum sat on her haunches as she entered and wagged her tail. Hannah settled down next to the dog and restowed her firearm. "Sorry to get everyone worked up."

"Don't apologize." Bruce laid his gun down before sitting at her side. "Like Trey said, it's better to be aware."

She gave him that smile. The one she used before making a joke. "He said to be frosty—not exactly a word from our generation."

"It's not," he agreed. "When I was Trey's age, frosty was something the windows got on cold nights."

"Or a frozen dessert."

"There's that, too." It was one more thing for him to like about Hannah. They were from the same era. "I was wondering if we should talk," he said. "You know, about the kiss."

She brushed dirt off the toe of her hiking boot. "I apologize if I made you uncomfortable. After the peck on the cheek, kissing you seemed like the next logical step." She looked up at him before dropping her gaze again. "I know you still care for your wife..."

This wasn't how Bruce wanted the conversation to go. He didn't know what to say next—or really at all. Before he could change his mind, he said, "I do still care for my wife. I always will. But being here, and with you, has made me realize something important."

She looked up at him. "What's that?"

"I want more out of life than I've recently given myself."

"And you got all of that from a kiss?"

It was more complicated than a single embrace. But Bruce hadn't parsed through his thoughts or feelings yet. "It was a nice kiss."

"I'm not looking for anything serious," said Hannah. "But if we make it back, maybe we should go to dinner or something."

"You mean a date?" Bruce never thought he'd want another woman after Pamela. Yet the idea of taking Hannah out made him happier than he'd been in years.

"I guess, if you want to call it a date. Sure. But we have to make it home first."

"We'll make it back." Bruce prayed that they'd both live long enough to get the chance. "And I will take you out on a date."

She smiled. "I'm keeping you to your promise."

Chapter 11

The second full day of their manhunt ended as the sun dipped below the horizon. As the trio made camp for another night, Hannah was surprised they'd all survived for this long. Aside from avoiding Decker Newcombe, they'd had to contend with the dangerous heat.

As dusk turned to night, they shared a small dinner of granola bars and trail mix. The food was welcome, but Hannah's stomach contracted painfully with hunger. What's more, she didn't know when she'd get a proper meal again.

She had kibble for two days stowed in her pack. She gave Gypsum a smaller serving than the dog usually ate. As her canine companion watched her with sad eyes, she knew that the dog was as unhappy with the situation as Hannah was. Running her hand over the Lab's fur, she said, "It'll be okay, girl. We'll be home tomorrow."

As he had earlier in the day, Trey offered to take the first watch.

This left Hannah and Bruce alone in the tent. Lying on her side, she curled into a ball and shivered. For ease of movement, they'd left much of their gear—including the sleeping bags—behind. There was no way they could start a fire—not unless they wanted Decker to find them. It meant there was nothing to keep the cold night air from seeping into her bones.

"Are you okay?" Bruce asked, his voice carrying in the silence of the night.

"Just cold," she said.

"Here." She could see his silhouette against the darkness. He removed his flannel shirt. "You can have this."

"I can't take that from you," she said.

"Really, take it. I sleep hot anyway. Most of the time, I'm just in my boxers."

The image of Bruce sprawled out on her bed in just his skivvies came to mind with such clarity that Hannah's face flushed so brightly she feared she would start to glow. She also started to sweat. If she was lucky, it'd lead to a hot flash. "I'm okay," she said. "Honestly."

"All right then," he said. "Sleep now. I'll take the next watch. If everything goes well, we'll be back at the vehicle before noon tomorrow."

"The problem is that nothing has gone well so far."

"I can't tell if you're kidding or not."

To be fair, she wasn't sure if she was trying to make a joke. "It's just a fact. Five of us came in for one man. Now, we're down to three people. I don't bet, but I'd say that the odds are in Decker's favor."

"We'll make it back." In the dark, he reached for her hand. "I promise."

Hannah didn't dare turn to look at him. But if she did, what would she see?

"Can I ask you a question?" Without waiting for an

answer, she continued. "How'd you get the scar at the back of your neck?"

"Oh, that." Bruce chuckled. "The rodeo came through Mercy every year. But that was decades ago. Anyway, they had an amateur bronc riding competition with prize money for the winner."

She knew where the story was going, even without the ending. She groaned. "Oh no."

"Oh yes," he said. "I've spent my whole life around horses. So, I figured, what the hell. The bronc did not care that I'd worked with a lot of other animals. He threw me in about two seconds. Busted my nose and sliced open the back of my head when I landed. Got seven stitches on my scalp and a good story out of my one rodeo."

The flush from her face cooled and the sweat that dampened her chest turned icy against her skin. She trembled again.

"You really are freezing," said Bruce. "You should take my shirt, really."

"If you give me a minute, I might get a hot flash," she joked. The hot flashes were anywhere from annoying to debilitating. But right now, she could use some internal fire.

"Come here," said Bruce, his voice like a wisp of smoke. "I can keep you warm."

She didn't resist as he moved closer and pressed his body against her side. His breath washed over her cheek. Her heart started racing and a delicious feeling spread from her middle.

"How's that?" he asked.

"This is perfect," she said, choosing her words carefully.

"Good," he said. "I'm glad."

That's when he placed his lips on hers. Hannah didn't want to overthink anything. She didn't want to worry about his feelings for his deceased wife. She also didn't want to worry about the danger of Decker—after all, Trey was standing guard. Giving in to the moment, she parted her lips. Bruce slipped his tongue into her mouth and pulled her closer, pressing her to him. She could feel the muscles of his chest and abs through the fabric of the clothing. He was close but she wanted him closer.

Wrapping her arms around his neck, she kissed him back. Exploring. Tasting.

Her fingers trailed through his hair and down his neck. She traced the muscles of his shoulders and arms. Bruce blazed a trail of kisses from her mouth to her cheek to her throat. He placed a single kiss at the top of her chest.

Lacing his fingers through the hem of her shirt, he lifted the fabric. Cool air kissed her skin. His fingers trailed a path from her stomach to her ribs, her chest, her breasts. Bruce traced her nipple through the fabric of her bra and Hannah kissed him harder.

She shifted onto her back, so he was hovering over her. Hannah spread her thighs and Bruce nestled between her legs. Through the fabric of his jeans, he was hard. Tilting her pelvis, she rubbed against him.

Hannah was an adult woman, and she knew what she wanted. And she did want Bruce.

Was she willing to take him as a lover? Here and now?

That's when Trey's voice came out of the silence. "Hey, you!" he yelled. "Stop or I'll shoot." It was followed by the sound of feet pounding against the ground.

Sitting back on his heels, Bruce called out, "What is it?"

"I see him," said Trey. "That bastard tried to sneak into camp and then he ran off."

Hannah sat up and reached for her backpack. Removing the gun, she said, "We have to help him."

Bruce already held the shotgun, and he exited the tent. Hannah followed. Outside, she stood and looked around. There was nothing to see but shadows, a sliver of moon and a million stars.

"Where is he?" she asked. "Where'd Trey go?"

"Damned if I know," said Bruce. "But we'll be ready if Decker tries to come back."

Trey had a visual on the killer, just a shadowy figure running through the darkness. He sprinted after him, knowing full well he'd been lucky to catch a glimpse of Decker. Now, if his luck held, Trey would be the one to finally apprehend the infamous murderer.

He liked the idea of being the one to make the arrest. Same as all the other victims, his former coworkers deserved justice. It didn't matter that he hadn't worked with Ezra or Slade for long. They'd been his teammates, and it was his duty to avenge their deaths.

As he ran, Trey removed a flashlight from one of the pockets on his pants. He attached a light to the barrel of his gun. He trained the beam on the killer's back. Stopping, he aimed and pulled the trigger. There was a staccato of gunfire, a burst of flames from the muzzle, and a chunk of rock exploded.

Trey's shot had been close, but was it enough to take down the disreputable Decker Newcombe? Trey stepped forward. Slowly. Carefully. Leveling the gun, he stepped around the boulder.

There was nothing and no one.

Shining his light, he scanned the darkness. The beam caught a reflective patch on the coat Decker wore. The killer was running again. This time, Trey wouldn't let him escape.

The light jerked and swayed with each of Trey's footfalls. Yet he kept the beam centered on Decker's back. Pushing his legs, he ran faster. His thighs ached. His head throbbed. His chest was tight and burned with each breath. But there was no way that he'd stop now.

Decker darted around the side of a bush. Trey lost sight of him, but only for a second. Taking the corner, he followed the killer.

There was a blur and a biting pain on the side of his head. He heard the crack of wood. Splinters clung to his skin as blood poured from his scalp. His vision wavered and turned fuzzy at the edges. Without question, he'd been hit in the face with a big stick. And he knew another thing to be true, as well: Decker had set up an ambush and Trey's confidence had let him fall into the trap.

He would've cursed, but his lips had already started to swell. His eyes watered. He lifted his rifle, ready to aim and fire. But Decker was gone.

"Focus, dammit. Focus."

Another limb crashed into the back of his head, forcing Trey to his knees. That's when he felt the cold steel of a barrel at the back of his head. "Give me your gun."

Trey hesitated. Without his weapon, he was nothing.

Decker pressed the barrel harder into his skull. "Give me your gun now."

Muttering a curse, Trey unhooked the strap and handed over the rifle.

Decker jerked it from his hands. "Now, give me the keys to your car. You do what I tell you, and I'll let you live."

Trey didn't believe the killer, but what choice did he have? Sticking his hand in his pocket, he reached for the keys. They weren't there. Velcro kept the pocket flaps closed. The keys couldn't have fallen out while he was running, could they? Well, if they had, then everyone was screwed.

That's when he remembered. After taking the keys from his pocket, he had held them out to Bruce. *Take these*, he'd said. *Keep them in your backpack. They're safer with you—at least while I'm on watch.*

Bruce had stowed them in his bag. The thing was, Trey hadn't bothered to get them back. He wanted to laugh. It was ironic, really, that he was going to die for nothing.

No, Trey wasn't ready to die.

And he definitely wasn't going to let Decker Newcombe be the one to kill him. He needed a plan. It's just that his head hurt too damn much to think.

Yet he raised his hands in surrender and said, "I don't have them with me. You're out of luck, pal."

"You're lying. Stand up." Decker's voice was steely

and sharp, like a dagger shoved into his ear. "And don't call me *pal*."

Trey stood. Decker approached and patted each of the pockets. The stench of body odor and death clung to the killer like a fog. Stepping back, Decker pointed the shotgun at his chest. "Where are the damn keys?"

"I told you. I don't have them."

"Where are they?"

Despite the pain in his head that throbbed with each beat of his heart, Trey knew what to do. "I think I lost them when I was chasing you."

"You what?" Decker asked, his eyes wide and his voice filled with incredulity. "How'd that happen?"

"If I knew," said Trey, knowing his words were full of snark, "I wouldn't have let them fall out of my pocket."

"Smart-ass." Decker slammed the butt on the rifle into Trey's belly. The blow knocked all the wind from his lungs. Dropping to his knees, Trey felt the granola bar and trail mix start to come up. But he'd be damned before he puked in front of the likes of Newcombe.

Trey knelt on the ground. There was a biting pain in his knee from a wound he didn't remember getting. No, it wasn't just an ordinary injury. He was kneeling on a rock, a big one—maybe the size of a dinner plate. Wheezing more than he needed, he dug his fingers around the side of the stone. He'd only have one chance and if he missed, it was game over.

The thing was, he didn't intend to miss.

Gasping once more, he raised a single hand. "Okay, you got me. I dropped the keys on purpose," he lied. He wasn't sure if the killer would believe him—after all, it wasn't the best story. "I didn't want to have them with me them in case we ended up like this."

"I don't believe you." Decker narrowed his eyes. "Why would you do something like that?"

Dammit. Now he had to sell the story. "The guy who got away from that massacre—his name was Warner Crane. He heard you demanding the car keys from his buddies. He was the one who had them. But I had to ask myself why you would risk everything to follow us—even after you took all our food?" The killer watched him, his expression neutral. Was he buying Trey's lie? "It had to be the keys, so I pitched them out of my pocket."

"Where'd you leave them?" asked Decker.

"I can't give you directions," he said. "But I can find them again."

The killer twitched the rifle. "Get up, nice and slow."

"Just a minute," he said, wheezing like he was weak and defeated. It was all an act. "I just need a minute to catch my breath."

"You don't have a minute," said Decker. "Get up. Now."

Rocking back to his heels, Trey picked up the stone. Marshaling all the strength in his shoulder, he held tight to the rock and swung it up like a shield. The stone hit the barrel of the gun.

It knocked the firearm up and back and left Decker's chin exposed. Trey wasn't about to give up. Holding onto the rock's edges, he shoved his hands forward. This time, he connected with Decker's chest. The killer staggered backward. Trey swung the rock again. At the same moment, Decker ducked. The rock only grazed the top of his head.

Trey wanted to curse. He needed to land a single, powerful blow. Or get the gun. He reached for the barrel and pulled the firearm toward him. Decker held the stock with both hands. Neither man was willing to let go. They wrestled for the rifle. Sweat streamed down Trey's face, stinging his eyes and leaving the taste of salt on his lips. But he wasn't going to give up.

Without warning, there was a shot. A flash of light and a boom, like thunder.

Blood covered Trey's hands. Someone had been hit. But where had the bullets gone?

A burst of gunfire echoed off the hills. Hannah felt the concussion of each bullet in her teeth. It was the second set of shots fired since Trey had spotted Decker.

I see him. That bastard tried to sneak into camp and then he ran off.

Gypsum whined. Holding tight to the leash, she kept the dog close to her side.

"Sounds like a semiautomatic rifle," said Bruce. He stood at her side and his arm brushed against her shoulder. "It's the same kind of weapon that Trey was carrying."

"So, he just shot Decker?" Hannah wanted to hope that the killer was finally dead. But she knew enough not to underestimate Decker Newcombe.

"We don't know what happened out there." Bruce held his shotgun across his chest with his finger hooked around the trigger guard. "All we can do is wait and be ready for anything." He paused a beat. "Get your backpack. Mine, too. If things went badly for Trey, we'll need to leave, and we won't have time to get our stuff."

Icy terror clawed Hannah's throat. "You think that Decker shot Trey?"

"I don't know what happened. But I do know we have to be ready for anything," he said again.

Bruce was right. And besides, she couldn't give in to the fear. She needed to focus on one task and then the next. And then the one after that. With Gypsum trailing behind her, she returned to the tent and retrieved both backpacks.

Dropping both packs to the dirt, she asked Bruce, "Do you see anything?"

"There's whole lotta nothing out there," he said with a shake of his head. He glanced at her. "You still got that gun?"

"It's stowed in the bag."

"Take it out and be ready to shoot at anything that moves. I'm going to put on my pack."

She held the firearm like she'd been taught. One hand on the trigger and the other on the grip. She kept her gaze trained on the darkness, but there was nothing to see. Bruce set his shotgun on the ground and donned his backpack.

"Now you," he said. "Put on your pack."

She set the gun next to her feet and picked up her backpack. After slipping her arms though the shoulder straps, she secured the chest and belly straps. Retrieving her firearm, she asked, "What do we do now?"

"Pray that Trey was the one who fired that gun."

Time seemed to stretch out, mere seconds passing like hours. Then she caught the crunch of footfalls on the rocky ground. "You hear that?"

"Sure do." Bruce lifted the shotgun and looked into the scope. "I can see someone. But I don't have night vision, so I can't see any features. They're moving slow. Casual." He paused. "They're wearing a white T-shirt. I think it's Trey."

Hannah exhaled. "Is this nightmare really over?"

Lowering his gun, Bruce glanced in her direction. "I think so." He smiled quickly and placed his lips on her forehead. "Now that Trey's shot Decker, I have to be honest. I wasn't sure if we were going to make it back home."

Before she could say anything, Gypsum let out a deep bark. The hair at the Lab's scruff stood on end. What did her dog know that she didn't?

Then she saw the man. He wore a white, long-sleeved T-shirt; the bright color was stark against the night. It was the same thing Trey had been wearing. But was it him? Hannah watched the man. His movements weren't right—this guy was loose where Trey was controlled. He wasn't as tall as Trey, either. Her stomach dropped to her shoes. Lifting her own gun, she took aim. "Bruce. That's not him."

Bruce leveled his shotgun at the killer. "Stop right there. Put down your weapon."

The man took two more steps. He was less than ten yards away. She could see him clearly now. He had a scraggly beard and long hair. Pulling on her lead, Gypsum barked. She pulled the dog back as the man stared at Hannah with his icy blue eyes. She couldn't help it, she shivered.

"I don't want any trouble," said Decker. "I just want the keys to your car. I'll let you keep your phones. You can call Texas Law and that lying bastard, Ryan Steele, to get you. But by then, I'll be gone."

"That's a lot of negotiating for man who I've got in my sights," said Bruce.

Decker sighed. "We've all got guns."

"You want to talk, put your rifle on the ground."

Decker set Trey's rifle next to his feet and raised his hands in surrender. "Give me your car keys. That's all I want. Hand them over and you'll never see me again."

"Where's Trey?" she asked.

"I'll make you a trade," said the killer. "The keys for your friend."

"Where is he?" asked Bruce.

"He's close by."

"How do we know he's not dead already?" Hannah challenged. "You killed Ezra—and Slade, too. Don't deny it."

"I'm not denying anything," said the killer. "I killed them both. I snuck up on blond guy and pushed him over the cliff. Getting rid of the second guy was a little harder. He put up a fight. But I had a knife when he was only worried about the gun."

His confession filled Hannah with loathing. She wanted to vomit just being in his presence. "You're vile," she said.

Gypsum tensed and gave a low growl. Hannah wrapped the lead tighter around her hand.

"I've been called a lot worse," said the killer. "But how you feel about me doesn't change anything. If you want Trey, you have to give me the keys to your vehicle."

"Prove to us that he's alive," demanded Bruce. "And then we'll talk."

"You want Trey." The killer slipped a pack from his back. "You got him."

He threw the bag. It landed with a thud next to Hannah's feet. A misshapen ball rolled out of the open compartment.

Except…it wasn't a ball. Trey's severed head lay at her feet. Eyes wide and mouth open, he stared at her in the middle of a silent scream.

Bile rose in the back of her throat and her hands went cold. Her arms trembled. The gun shook. Fire erupted from the muzzle. The recoil shoved her, and she stumbled backward. Gypsum lunged, pulling Hannah further off balance. She stumbled and righted herself.

At the same moment, Decker dove for the rifle he'd dropped at his feet. He pulled the trigger. The earth at Hannah's ankles exploded as bullets tore through the backpack and Trey's severed head.

Bruce fired his shotgun once. There was a deafening boom. The scent of gunpowder filled the night. A cloud of smoke wafted from the barrel. When the smoke cleared, the killer was gone.

Chapter 12

Bruce kept the rifle tight into his shoulder and aimed at the spot where Decker had been standing. Slowly, carefully, he took several steps forward. On the ground was a dark pool. Kneeling, he touched the soil. It was warm and smelled of copper and gore. Without question, it was blood. There was a drop of blood and then another. The trail led into the desert. "I'm going after him," he said, filled with a steely resolve as he straightened. "I shot him. It won't take long to catch him and finish off that bastard."

"Are you kidding?" Hannah pulled him around to face her. "We don't know if that blood is even Decker's. It might be Trey's. All of this might be a trick." Her voice broke on the last word. "Going after him might be exactly what he wants."

The need to avenge all of Decker's victims was like a powerful thirst. But Hannah had a point. He'd decapitated Trey as a horrific diversion so he could kill them, too.

It meant there was only one thing to do.

"C'mon," he said, starting to walk. "We've got to get

back to the vehicle. We'll pick up cellular coverage before we make it to the SUV."

Hannah jogged to catch up. Her dog was at her side. As they walked, she reached for him, placing her hand on his arm. Her touch was warm and strong and left him wanting more. But he didn't have the mental or emotional space to think about a future when he wasn't even sure if they'd survive the night.

Decker sat on the ground and used a rock as a chair-back. His arm felt as if it had been set on fire. The once-white T-shirt was now black with blood. The sleeve was wet and stuck to the wound on his biceps. Peeling back the fabric, he looked at the injury. With each beat of his heart, gore pumped out of a hole in his arm. His hand was numb.

But if he wanted to survive, he had to stop the bleeding.

Decker worked his shoulder out of the shirt. He pulled the sleeve off his wounded arm and then over his head. His eyes stung, sweat coated his flesh. The night air was cold, and he began to shiver.

Holding the shirt's hem in his teeth, he ripped off a strip of cloth. He tied the band tight to his arm. For a moment, bright spots exploded in his vision. Leaning back, he waited until his vision cleared.

His hand was still numb, and blood covered his arm. Using the rest of the fabric, he wiped away the gore. Decker had more clothes from the group of men he'd killed. He worked his injured arm into a jacket and pulled the zipper up to his chin. He used a pair of pants to make a bulky sling. At least it took pressure off his injured arm.

He wanted to sit. To rest. To recover.

But he couldn't wait for long. He had to figure out where the last two survivors were going. More than needing their vehicle, if he truly wanted to escape, he could leave no witnesses.

The man and woman had to die.

Hannah and Bruce walked through the dark. With each step, she could feel Decker's eyes on her back. He was out there, she knew, and he wasn't going to stop until they were dead. Yet each step was also a small victory. It was one step closer to the SUV. One step farther from the shoot-out with Decker. Since they were taking a straight route back to the SUV, the walk would be shorter. But in the dark, it was no less treacherous. She trusted Bruce to know where he was going and to know what they were doing. But her pulse raced, and her skin prickled with anxiety.

They hadn't decided to keep quiet, but she knew that talking would be a mistake. Decker could hear them from more than a quarter of a mile away. Idle chitchat might mean the difference between life and death. At her side, Gypsum walked, sniffing the ground and panting.

One more step. Another. And another.

Eventually, she knew they'd walked more than a mile. But how much farther did they have to go?

As they trudged up the side of a hill, she couldn't stand the silence any longer. "Do you know where we are?"

"We're getting close," said Bruce. He removed a bottle of water from his bag and held it out to Hannah. Her fingertips brushed the back of his hand and, despite the circumstances, her heart skipped a beat. "By the time we climb the next rise, we should pick up a clear cell signal."

After unscrewing the lid, she drank a swallow of water and held out the bottle to Bruce. As he took a drink, she glanced into the night. There was another hill in the distance. "How long will it take us to get over there?"

"It's another few miles. Maybe two hours of walking. Maybe a little less." And then he said, "Give me Gypsum's dish. We'll let her get a drink, too. You and I can use a rest."

Hannah removed the collapsible bowl from her bag and set it on the ground. Bruce emptied the bottle, and they stood in silence as the dog lapped up the water. There was already a long catalog of things that she liked about Bruce. But she added the fact that he was kind to animals—especially her dog—to that list.

The dog licked the last drops of water from the bowl. Hannah picked it up from the ground and folded it flat before putting it into her bag. "You ready?" she asked.

"Let's go," he said.

The dark surrounded them, and the night seemed endless. Yet she could see enough to follow Bruce down the hill. She was careful about where she stepped. Hannah didn't know what might be underfoot. A loose rock. A hole. A snake.

No. She had to focus on getting home. She pictured the house she'd purchased. The bright, white kitchen filled with sun. The living room, with cozy chairs. She saw herself curled up on the sofa, Gypsum dozing on the floor by her feet. Bruce was there, too, sitting at her side with his hand in hers.

Nothing else mattered.

The valley between the two hills was wide and they walked for more than an hour. Her mouth was dry. Hunger gnawed at her stomach. Her legs ached and her feet throbbed with each step. The straps of her backpack dug into her shoulders and turned the skin near her pits raw. She was used to physical activity, but this was more strain than she'd ever endured.

What else was she going to do? Lie down and die? Or wait for the killer to find her? Just like the little locomotive from her childhood book, she moved forward.

At the top of the hill, Bruce stopped. "We'll take another break," he said, "and see if there's any signal for the phone."

Hannah found a bottle of water in her backpack. After taking a drink, she filled Gypsum's bowl again and saved the last of the water for Bruce. He'd taken his phone from his bag and was waiting for the device to power up.

"Three bars," he said. "We should be able to make a call."

She stood at his side as he pulled up his contact list. He selected Ryan Steele's number and placed the call. The phone started to trill, the sound loud in the silent desert.

Hannah held her breath and counted the rings. One. Two. Three. Four. The liquid in her empty stomach gurgled. They couldn't have come this far only to have their call go unanswered.

After the fifth ring, a sleepy voice said, "Hello? Bruce, is that you?"

"Hey, man. I'm happy to hear your voice. We've had some setbacks," said Bruce, "and we need help."

"Setbacks? Help? What happened?" Even with the phone pressed to his ear, Hannah could hear Ryan's voice.

Bruce gave a quick rundown of everything that had happened over the past two days.

"Listen," said Bruce. "We're heading back to the vehicle, but we don't know where Decker is now. I shot him. We found the blood trail. But we didn't investigate."

"How far are you from your vehicle?" Ryan asked.

"It'll take us another hour to get there," said Bruce.

Good God. Another hour of walking? To Hannah, that felt like days.

On the other end of the call, Ryan cursed. "Okay. We'll rendezvous there," he said. "It might take us that long to get to you."

"Got it," said Bruce before ending the call. He turned to Hannah.

"Well," she said. "I guess we should get going."

She tried to sound upbeat. But Hannah knew that in the hills, and with a killer on the loose, an hour was an eternity.

Decker followed the man and woman from a distance. He'd heard enough of their conversations to know that her name was Hannah and his name was Bruce. For some reason, he liked knowing their names. It gave him some control that he lacked if his victims were nameless.

He'd heard the phone call and knew they were headed to the vehicle. He also knew that Ryan and his newfound friends at Texas Law were on their way. He had to get to the car before the couple made it back. But with his wounded arm, could he?

Decker drank a bottle of water and ate spaghetti from a pouch. The food helped to give him energy. But his arm still throbbed. He opened and closed his fist. His palm filled with pinpricks of pain as blood circulated through his hand. Hoisting the backpack onto his good shoulder, Decker hooked both guns onto his belt. He began to walk. The firearms slapped his thighs with each step. He'd have bruises come morning, but for now, it couldn't be helped.

As he walked, his mind wandered back to when he was a kid. He and Ryan Steele had borrowed a tent from one of Ryan's uncles and taken it to the woods near their trailer park. They'd camped out that night, pretending to be explorers in the jungle. They'd heated baked beans over an open fire and eaten them straight out of the can. It was one of the few times that Decker remembered being happy.

Decker had told Ryan he had a plan—a way to make money so they would never be poor again. At first, Ryan seemed reluctant to go along. *Hurting people wasn't right*, he'd said. It didn't matter if they got paid to do it. But Decker had persisted. "You could make money and pay for your own college." Finally, it seemed like Ryan was relenting.

"We have to make a pact—to swear to each other—that we will always have each other's back."

"Sure," Ryan had said, shrugging his slight shoulders. "I swear."

Decker knew he hadn't meant it. "We have to do something better. Something more."

He'd convinced Ryan to give him his pocketknife.

"We're going to make a blood oath." He'd opened the blade and sliced his own palm. He remembered that the pain felt like he'd caught a bolt of lightning with his hand. The flaps of skin had separated for an instant. Then the seam had filled with blood. "Give me your hand."

Ryan had balled his palm into a fist. "No way are you going to cut me. It'll hurt."

"It doesn't hurt. Baby. Chicken." He'd started to cluck, knowing full well that the taunting would work.

"Fine." Ryan had stretched out his arm.

He'd unfurled his friend's fingers. The blade had glinted in the firelight as he'd drawn the knife edge down the middle of the other boy's palm.

"Dammit. You lied. That does hurt."

Decker recalled looking at the wound on his friend's palm and feeling euphoria the likes of which he'd never before experienced. The pain. The blood.

The moment was nothing short of religious for him. "Now we have to shake," he'd said.

Ryan had held out his hand. The blood was smeared across his palm, so dark that it looked black in the firelight. A quickening had started up in Decker's middle, unfurling until it filled his veins. Grabbing his friend's wrist, he'd pressed their cuts together. "Now," he'd said. "We're blood brothers. Together forever."

"Together forever." For a moment, neither had spoken. Then Ryan had asked, "You got a bottle of water or something? I gotta wash my hand. All this blood is gross."

Decker had held out a bottle. "Here you go."

Ryan rinsed his hand, cleaning the cut. He'd wiped his damp palm on the leg of his jeans.

That's the moment Decker had known he was different.

When Ryan had seen the cut, he'd thought it gross. A wound that needed to be cleaned and tended. Decker, on the other hand, had been excited by the blood. The gore. The injury. The pain. He'd seen the beauty in destruction. He'd known then the trajectory of his life, even if he hadn't known the exact steps he would need to take. He'd just known he would be an artist, and that death would be his medium.

As he walked, the sky started to lighten, Decker rubbed the center of his palm. The scar was still on his flesh and yet the only thing that hurt now was the betrayal from his friend.

Decker was a survivor. Hell, he was the ancestor of Jack the Ripper. Deep in his soul, he knew that he was destined for greatness. In his bones, he knew that he'd survive. He had so much yet to accomplish. One day, he'd be more famous than his ancestor. But there were things Decker needed to take care of first. Scores that he needed to be settled. Taking care of Ryan was only the beginning.

Chapter 13

Hannah had survived the night. The eastern horizon was filled with pinks and purples and oranges as a new day began. She didn't dare hope too much. All the same, she could feel it in her bones—they'd escaped the killer. Dragging in a deep breath, she passed the leash from one hand to the other.

"The SUV's not far from here," said Bruce.

"Finally, our luck changed. We made it."

Shifting his shotgun so it was even with his hip, Bruce looked over his shoulder. "We haven't made it yet. Right now, we need to be careful."

"Careful?" Hannah had all but convinced herself that they were going to be safe. "Decker might've gotten seriously hurt when you shot him. Hell, he might be dead."

"I don't hold a lot of stock in might be." He glanced at her and smiled quickly. "No offense."

Hannah wasn't offended. But she was exhausted and didn't have any emotional space to be careful or vigilant. As the sky lightened, it was easier to see her surroundings. They had walked to the base of a hill. She remembered coming down the same side they now had to climb. "It feels like Ryan asked me to join the search party weeks earlier, not two days ago."

They climbed to the top of the hill as the first rays of sun broke over the horizon. The light glinted off the roof of the SUV. They had less than a quarter of a mile to walk. Their nightmare was almost over. Wind blew, pulling a strand of hair out of her bun. Bruce reached over and tucked the hair behind her ear.

"Maybe you're right," he said. "Maybe Decker's died from his wounds." He was quiet for a moment. "I never killed anyone before. I don't regret it—I don't think. I mean, it was him or us."

Taking a few steps, she searched for the right words. Nothing came to her. "I wish I knew what to say."

He shook his head. "There's nothing to say," he conceded, his words carried away by the wind. Turning his face skyward, he noted, "I think a storm is brewing."

Another gust of wind blew, sending a spiral of dust skittering across the ground. She looked up. Fat, gray clouds roiled above her. He was right. A storm was coming in. But they'd be in the SUV and long gone before the first drop of rain fell.

She glanced down at Gypsum. The dog's tongue hung out of her mouth and her lips were turned up in a smile. The canine could tell that they were almost home.

"So," said Bruce. The SUV was less than two hundred yards away. "Any idea where you want to go on our date?"

Their date. When he'd asked her out, it seemed like they'd never make it. But they had.

"I just moved to town," she said. "You decide what we should do."

"I was thinking that maybe we could go for a walk in Hill Country."

After the past forty-eight hours, it was the last thing she wanted to do. Then she realized. "You're joking. Right?"

"Right," he said. After a moment, he added, "Maybe you can come to my place. I make a good shepherd's pie."

It had been an entire day since she'd eaten a meal—and that had come out of a packet. "Right now," she said, "I'd eat almost anything. But I'd love to come over to your house for dinner."

He nodded once. "Tuesday night?"

"I'll bring dessert."

"Then it really is a date."

"The keys," said Hannah. "You have them, right?"

"They're in my bag." Dropping his backpack to the ground, he unfastened the zipper and knelt in the dirt. After shifting the rifle to his back, where it hung by the strap, he sifted through his gear. A moment later, he stood. The fob was in his hand. "Got it."

That's when Decker Newcombe stepped out from behind the SUV. The killer held Trey's semiautomatic rifle. The barrel was aimed at Hannah's chest. "I'll take those keys, if you don't mind. Just throw them on the ground and I'll be on my way."

"And what if I don't?" asked Bruce.

She appreciated his bluster, but what were they going to do? She had a gun, but it was stowed in the webbing on her pack. Bruce's shotgun was on his back—easier to reach than her own pistol—but he wouldn't be quicker than a bullet.

"You know I'm going to get those keys from you," said the killer. "The question is—do you want to die before I take them?"

Bruce paused. "If I give you these, you have to promise not to kill Hannah or her dog."

"You aren't in a place to negotiate with me. I'm the one with the guns, remember?"

Bruce pressed a button on the fob. The lights flashed and the locks unlatched with a click. "Go ahead," he said. "Get in the SUV. Let Hannah and her dog walk away. Once they're safe, I'll give you the fob."

That's when she realized something important. Bruce didn't expect to survive. By trying to save her life, he was sacrificing his own.

"Bruce, no." She reached for his wrist. The cords of muscle in his arms were like bands of iron. "There's something else we can do..."

"I'm glad we met," he said, placing a kiss on her cheek. "Just go back the way we came. If I don't come for you, you know that Texas Law is on the way. They'll be here soon. You'll be fine."

Her eyes burned and emotion clogged her throat. How could he be so calm at a time like this? "I won't... I can't..." Her voice cracked on the last word.

"You can and you will," said Bruce. "Tell Shana that I love her, okay?"

A large tear rolled down her cheek. She wiped it away, but the salt clung to her lips. "Bruce, don't do this—"

"The keys," said Decker. "Or I shoot you all and then your tearful goodbye won't matter."

Like a switch had been flipped, Hannah went from despondent to enraged. In two days, Decker had murdered three operatives from Texas Law. He'd snuffed out their lives with as much thought as blowing out a candle. She couldn't let him take one more life.

"Go, Hannah. Please."

She squeezed Bruce's arm once more. "Be safe. You still owe me a shepherd's pie."

He gave her a wan smile. "Ryan and the rest will be here soon."

Hannah refused to cry or beg. Even if she did, she doubted that the killer would listen. They'd been playing cat and mouse since walking into this wretched grassland. He'd been the last to lay a trap. But the game wasn't over. She let her arm out of one loop of the backpack and started walking toward the hill. She counted her steps. At fifty paces, she glanced over her shoulder.

Bruce tossed the keys to Decker. The killer bent down to retrieve them before standing straight. She wasn't being watched and knew that now was her time.

Bruce wasn't ready to meet his Maker. He didn't want to see his wife again—or not yet at least. But he'd do anything to save Hannah, including making the ultimate sacrifice. Bracing his feet against the ground, he held his breath. For a moment, he wondered how much it would hurt to be shot. Would he have a clean death—where he was alive one minute and gone the next? Or would Decker shoot him in the gut, leaving him with several agonizing minutes of bleeding out?

So the report from the gun didn't surprise him. But in the seconds after the weapon was fired, he expected something to hurt. Or for his shirt to be covered in blood. But there was nothing. And then he saw it. Bright and red, blood bloomed on Decker's side. Turning pale, he staggered backward.

"Son of a bitch," the killer snarled as he lifted his own firearm.

Bruce glanced over his shoulder. Hannah was standing there, with a gun in her hand. A tendril of smoke rose from the barrel. She'd fired on the killer. But now, Decker aimed his own rifle at her. With a roar, Bruce launched himself from where he stood. He grabbed Decker around the middle and pulled him to the ground.

Bruce slammed his fist into Decker's face. Once. Twice. Three times. With each hit, he mentally said a name. Slade. Ezra. Trey. His knuckles throbbed and blood spurted from the murderer's nose.

Decker lifted his rifle. Bruce pinned his wrist to the ground. The killer still writhed. It was like wrestling with a snake. But just like with any snake he'd ever caught, Bruce refused to let go.

He dug his fingers into the flesh on Decker's wrist. The killer screamed in pain and bucked, lifting Bruce off the ground. It was just enough leverage for Decker to work his feet free. He kicked Bruce in the face. For a moment, white dots filled his vision.

There was a boom as a blast of fire and smoke escaped from the muzzle. Like he'd been punched by God,

Bruce was knocked back to the dirt. He looked at his chest. A dark red stain was blooming on his own shirt. He'd been shot; he knew it.

Decker stumbled forward and scooped up the keys. He pulled open the driver's-side door and within seconds, the engine revved. The tires kicked up dirt and gravel as the SUV sped away. Bruce stared at the taillights for a moment until his head became too heavy to hold up. He fell back as a thick cloud blotted out the sun.

He felt as if he were part of the cloud and floating above the earth. He watched from above as Hannah raced to his side.

"Bruce," she said, "don't you dare leave me."

She pressed a bandage to his chest, staunching the bleeding. In the distance, he heard the sound of several cars coming in fast. The roar of the motors. The crunch of the tires on gravel.

"They're coming," she said, shaking his shoulder. "The team from Texas Law is almost here. Don't you dare leave me." He pried his eyes open. Hannah's nose was inches from his own. "You and me, we have a date. Remember."

He raised his hand, even though it seemed to be made of lead, and placed it on her cheek. "I wish I'd met you sooncr."

Then the world closed in on all sides, and the cloud slipped away.

The operatives from Texas Law arrived just as Bruce lost consciousness. They'd come prepared with a well-stocked first aid kit and a nurse named Eva Tamke. She'd treated Bruce, bringing him to a stable condition. He'd been placed in a van that had been converted to an ambulance and rushed to the small hospital in Encantador for further treatment. It had taken everything in Hannah to not insist that she stay with him during the trip back to town. But she knew that she'd only get in the way if she tried to remain at Bruce's side.

Hannah, along with Ryan, had ridden in the dark SUV that followed the ambulance. During the ride, she'd told him everything about their time tracking Decker—including where the bodies of Slade and Ezra were buried. She also told him where to find Trey's head but could only guess where the body might have been left.

Once they returned to town, Ryan offered to take Hannah home. But she needed to know how Bruce was doing and asked to be taken to the hospital. For almost an hour, she'd sat in the waiting room. The scent of disinfectants and cold coffee hung in the air. Overhead, fluorescent lights buzzed. A TV hung on the wall. A cooking show was playing. The host chopped vegetables in preparation for making a shepherd's pie. Hannah felt the show was an omen. What she didn't know was if it was a good sign—or a bad one.

Gypsum lay on the floor and rested her head on Hannah's feet. Certainly, dogs weren't allowed in the hospital most of the time. But she assumed after everything that had happened, they'd made an exception for her.

During the hour of waiting, Hannah had eaten several packets of crackers and drank two cups of tea. Funny how she'd been starving only hours earlier. But now the snacks sat in her gut like a rock. A door opened and

Ryan Steele entered. Lines of worry were etched into his face. Hannah's throat closed at the sight of him. But he wasn't alone. With him was a blond man in suit pants, white shirt and a red tie. Pressing her back into the seat, she prepared to hear the worst news.

"Hey," Ryan said, sitting in the chair next to hers. He nodded toward the other man. "This is Jason Jones, he's with the FBI."

"I'm Hannah Jefferies. This is my search dog, Gypsum."

At the mention of her name, the canine lifted her head and thumped her tail against the floor.

Jason knelt in front of Gypsum. While stroking the back of the dog's neck, he said, "My brother, Marcus, had a chocolate Lab when we were growing up. He was supposed to be the family pet, but he loved my brother."

Hannah liked anyone who liked animals. "It's a good breed. Smart. Loyal. Loving." Then again, in her estimation, all dogs had those qualities. "How is he?" she asked, "Bruce, I mean."

"He's out of surgery. The bullet passed through his chest and, luckily, missed anything vital. The doctor here was able to fix everything. Right now, they're waiting for a medevac to take him to San Antonio Medical Center. There's a storm, so we don't know when they'll be here. But for now, Bruce is as good as can be expected."

Hannah let out a long breath. Her shoulders slumped, releasing the tension she'd been holding. "That's good news. Great news, really. Is he awake? Can I see him?"

Jason straightened and shrugged. "We just came from

his room. He's pretty drowsy, as you can imagine. But we'd like to talk to you about what you saw."

"Which time?"

"Start with the end," said Jason. "What do you remember about the last time you saw Decker?"

It didn't matter that she'd told her story several times during the ride to the hospital, she imagined that the FBI agent wanted to hear it from her directly. "Once I walked to the ridge, I pulled out my gun and shot Decker. I hit him in the side. He was bleeding when he stole the car, but I couldn't tell you how badly he'd been hurt." She paused. "You can track the vehicle, right? It has a GPS, or something."

"It looks like Decker snuck across the southern border and ditched the car. Like you said, he was hurt. We found a good bit of blood on the seats. It's going to be analyzed to see if the amount he lost is fatal," said Jason. "But, did he say anything about where he was going? Mention any names?"

"He didn't say anything about anyone else," said Hannah, certain in her memories. "He just wanted the keys to the SUV so badly, he was willing to kill."

Jason held out a business card. "If you think of anything else, even if it seems unimportant, call me."

She took the card and tucked it into the front pocket of her pants. She didn't think that anything more would come to her. Still, she said, "Will do."

"Bruce," she added. "Can I see him?"

Jason and Ryan exchanged glances. "I don't see why not. His daughter's with him now."

"He's on the second floor," Ryan told her. "Ask at the

nurses' station. They'll show you to his room. You want us to go with you?"

"I can find him," she said while getting to her feet. After hours of walking and then sitting, her legs were both stiff and numb. She stomped her feet, bringing blood back into her extremities. Slinging her bag over her shoulder, she tugged on the dog's leash and Gypsum rose, as well. With a small wave to the two men, she left the waiting room.

The medical facility in Encantador was a small hospital and an adjacent clinic that took up two stories. As she walked down the hallway, the salty scent of bacon and the earthy aroma of coffee came from the cafeteria. A clock hung on the wall. It was 9:07 a.m. It seemed like breakfast was still being served, and her stomach contracted painfully. Gypsum licked her chops, taking in the smell of food.

They both needed more to eat and a long rest. But first she needed to see Bruce and make sure that he was going to recover. A metal door stood at the end of the hall. It led to a stairwell, in which she took the steps two at a time to the second floor. Hannah exited through a similar metal door that led to another corridor.

The nurses' station was situated in the middle of the hallway. A young man with dark hair bleached blond at the ends stood behind a circular counter. He wore a name tag around his neck that read "Dennis Chen." He smiled as she approached. "Can I help you?"

"I'm here to see Bruce McDaniel." It occurred to her that she wasn't a family member. While Gypsum was a registered service dog, she wasn't in need of any assistance. Would she be told to leave the hospital? "I was with him in on the search." She glanced down at her canine companion. "We both were."

"He's in the third room on the left. His daughter is with him now."

Hannah had met Shana more than once. Yet, would she be overstepping her relationship with Bruce by interrupting father-and-daughter time?

No. She needed to see Bruce, even if it was just for a minute. Rolling back her shoulders, she walked down the corridor. The door was ajar, and she knocked lightly.

From inside the room, Shana called out, "Come in."

Hannah pushed open the door and crossed the threshold.

Shana sat in a chair that was shoved into the corner. Her blond hair was pulled into a ponytail. She wore a gray T-shirt and a pair of jeans. Bruce lay in the bed, his eyes closed. There was a large bandage wrapped around one shoulder and his chest. A white blanket was draped over his legs.

"Hey," said Hannah. "I'm sorry to bother you, I just wanted to check on your dad."

Shana rose and pulled Hannah in for a hug. "Thanks for sticking around to make sure he's okay." She released the embrace. "Actually, thanks for everything. Ryan and the fed haven't said much to me about what happened, but my dad has been fading in and out. He said that you saved his life."

"We took care of each other," she said.

Shana squeezed her arm. "I don't know how to thank you."

Hannah's fingers itched with the need to touch Bruce's hand. But she couldn't reach for him—not in front of Shana. "Well, I didn't want to interrupt what you're doing. I should probably..." She tilted her head toward the door. "You know, go."

"Can I ask you a favor? Can you hang out here with my dad? I need to get to the office and take care of a few things, but I don't want to leave him alone—not even for an hour." She paused before adding, "I can even take Gypsum with me. She can hang out at the office."

The dog needed a break. "Thanks. I think she'd like that."

Shana took the leash and hugged Hannah once more. "Thanks for everything."

Hannah sat in the seat Shana had just vacated. On the far side of his bed, a window was set into the wall. It was the first glimpse of daylight she'd caught since coming to the hospital. Water streaked down the pane as sheets of rain fell. The storm they'd predicted had finally arrived.

Bruce was hooked up to several monitors. His pulse, respiration and heart rate were all steady. An IV bag was hooked to a metal pole that sat at the bedside. Clear liquid dripped into a tube that wound to a needle inserted into a vein on the back of his hand. She reached for his fingertips and rubbed the backs of his knuckles. "Glad to see that you made it."

His eyelids fluttered and his lips moved, yet he made no sound.

"What'd you say?" she asked, moving closer.

Bruce spoke, his voice nothing more than a whisper. "I wouldn't miss our date for anything."

Chapter 14

For Bruce, life had been reduced to snapshots. The pain in his chest and shoulder. The weightlessness of watching his prone body on the ground. The bright lights from the operating room. Faces appeared and disappeared from his vision, as well, but he kept falling in and out of consciousness, struggling to remember who came and when. Except Hannah. He remembered seeing Hannah.

He realized that he was awake even before he opened his eyes. His throat was raw, and his mouth tasted like it'd been used as a garbage can. He coughed. Pain surged through his chest. He grimaced.

"Here," said a female voice. "Take a sip."

A straw was placed near his lips, and he sucked down cool water. He let the straw fall from his mouth and breathed deeply. A warm hand gripped his wrist. "Rest," soothed the woman.

Without thinking, he grabbed her fingertips and peeled his eyelids open. Hannah sat at the edge of his bed. "You're here," he said, the words coming out as a croak.

She smiled. "Shana and I have been taking turns sitting at your bedside. Sage has helped out, too." She squeezed his hand. "Speaking of Shana, she'll want to know that you're awake. I should call her, and let the doctor know."

She stood, but he held tight to her hand. "Wait a minute. What happened out there?"

"You were shot," she said, "by Decker. The bullet went through here." She pointed to the muscles between her shoulder and her chest. "It didn't hit anything important, and they did emergency surgery here in Encantador. At first, the doctors wanted to send you to San Antonio. But Shana thought it would be better if you stayed here so people could come and visit. And trust me, you've had a lot of visitors."

Bruce didn't like the idea of people staring at him while he lay helpless in the bed.

Something of his thoughts must've shone on his face. "I really should get the doctor. She can get you meds for the pain."

"Water," he said. "Can you get me another sip of water?" Bruce held on to her hand, forcing Hannah to twist in her seat to reach the cup. She held it to his lips as he drank again. He spit out the straw. "Thanks."

"I should…" she began.

He knew that she was right. Both the doctor and Shana needed to know that he was awake. But he wanted one more minute alone with Hannah. "Where's Decker now?"

She shook her head and let out a long breath. "He got away again. The SUV he stole was found in Mexico. There's drone footage of him crossing the southern border, but nothing of him exiting the vehicle. Since then, nothing's turned up. As far as law enforcement knows, Decker doesn't have any more contacts. He was shot and is in need of medical care. Obviously, he hasn't shown up at a hospital for treatment. There's a theory that he died of his wounds, but no body has been found..." She sighed again. "Basically, nobody knows anything."

Hannah's words washed over Bruce like a wave, leaving him dazed and breathless. Decker, the son of a bitch, had escaped again. Too many times, people had thought he was dead, and they'd been wrong.

She squeezed his fingers and rose. He knew he was going to have to let go of her hand this time. "I need to get the doctor," she told him, pulling away and walking to the door.

"Wait," he said as her fingertips slipped from his grasp. Until this very moment, Bruce had assumed that he'd just come out of surgery. But there were little clues in what Hannah told him that made him think his assumption was faulty. First, she had an awful lot of information for an investigation that was just a few hours old. He could also remember several folks stopping by to see him. "What day is it?"

"It's Thursday," she said. "Just a little after two in the afternoon."

"Thursday afternoon," he repeated in a whisper. The last thing he remembered was sunrise on Wednesday morning. "You mean to tell me that I've been out for an entire day?"

"Not completely out," she corrected. "They kept you sedated so you could heal. You could flutter your eyes a bit. Take sips of water. Squeeze the doctor's hand when they asked. You could talk a bit, but mostly you faded in and out." She nodded toward the door, still eager to let the doctor know that he was awake. Now he knew why she was so keen to tell someone. "I better get someone. Really."

"Wait," he said again, reaching out his hand. The movement pulled his opposite shoulder and pain zinged in his chest. He melted into the pillows and panted until the ache passed. "You've been here since Wednesday?"

She came back to his bedside and pressed her lips onto his forehead. "There's no place else I'd rather be."

Bruce watched her walk out of his room, admiring the view of her butt in a pair of jeans. He supposed that was a good sign that he felt well enough to appreciate an attractive woman. But Hannah wasn't just any woman. She was…well, he wasn't sure what she was to him. But he couldn't wait to see what happened next.

After a week of medical care, Bruce was ready to go home. He needed to get the stench of cleaner and rubbing alcohol out of his nose. The doctor had already signed the discharge papers, and he was waiting for Hannah to pick him up.

He wasn't going back to his house or to work right away. Instead, he'd be staying with Hannah until he could function alone full-time. If he were to be honest, Bruce was happy about the arrangement. Over the past week, Hannah had visited him every day. They'd watched TV, laughing at the same jokes. They'd played dozens of rounds of Uno and gin rummy. He'd even read a book from her book club—the first novel he'd read in years—and they'd discussed the story late into the night.

A treatment plan for his discharge from the hospital had been discussed several times. Bruce wasn't an invalid. He could feed himself, dress himself—with some help, of course. He could also walk up and down a flight of stairs. But after the trauma and surgery, the doctor felt it was best that Bruce not stay alone for a couple of weeks.

Hannah was the first person who came to mind. Sure, his daughter made sense. After all, she was family. But Shana's office was twenty minutes from her house. If he stayed with her, she'd have to take off from work to care for him. Hannah's training school was on her property. She could still see clients and check in on him regularly. Plus, Hannah had a larger house than Shana. The old farmstead had several bedrooms. Shana lived in the only condo complex in the area. Staying with his daughter meant that Bruce would have to crash in a home office that just so happened to have a bed.

But it was more than logistics. He wanted to be around Hannah all the time. He remembered feeling that way when he'd first started dating Pamela. It was bittersweet to know that he had truly moved into a new phase of his life. What's more, Bruce knew what all the emotions meant. Simply put, he was falling in love again.

Bruce had already donned his jeans. Sitting on the side of the bed, he slowly buttoned his plaid shirt. There was a knock at his door.

"Come in," he said, slipping the last button through the hole.

Both Hannah and Ryan Steele crossed the threshold.

Hannah's dark hair was loose, hanging in mahogany waves around her shoulders. She wore a blue sundress that hugged her breasts and hung loose around her hips. She also wore a pair of white sneakers, so bright that they reflected the overhead light.

"Wow," he said. "You look great."

"Thanks," said Ryan, smoothing down the front of his dark shirt. "I tried to dress up a little." As soon as he spoke, he laughed to show that he was joking. "But you're right—that dress looks nice on Hannah."

To Bruce, the word *nice* seemed like an understatement. Then again, Ryan was getting married in a few weeks. Keeping his compliments low-key was probably best.

Hannah swished the skirt of her dress. "I'm more of a jeans and T-shirt kind of gal. But I figured you getting out of the hospital was a big deal and decided to wear something nice."

So, she'd dressed up for him. Unbidden, a memory came to him. It was night and they were in the tent, in the desert. His lips were on her mouth. His body was above hers and his hips rested between her thighs. The desire to be inside her was a basic need. It was a hunger. A thirst. And now, he'd be staying at her house. Would their romance be renewed?

"I expected to see Hannah," he said, focusing on Ryan. "But I'm surprised to see you here. Hopefully, it's because you have news. Was Decker arrested? Or better yet, is he dead?"

"The FBI sent out a press release about your release

from the hospital today. A few media outlets have sent reporters. They called my office and asked to speak to you both. It's completely up to you," said Ryan. "But if you want to talk to the media, we can set up for a quick press conference, if you'd like."

Bruce didn't have any interest in talking to reporters. But the story of what had happened had become news—both locally and at the national level. The updates had aired constantly during commercial breaks while he and Hannah watched TV. "I'll do it," he said, knowing the only way to get rid of the media was to give them what they wanted. "But only on one condition. The two of you have to speak to the reporters with me."

"I've done my share of interviews—" Ryan began.

Before he could say anything else, Bruce interrupted. "Then you should be an old pro at this and will help us all look better."

He shrugged. "I'm game if Hannah is."

"I suppose we need to talk to them sometime."

"I'll find the hospital's administrator and see if we can use the conference room." Ryan crossed the small room and paused on the threshold. "Give me a minute and I'll be right back." Then he pushed the door open and walked into the hallway. The door swung back, closing with a click.

The sound echoed in Bruce's chest.

"So," he asked. "Are you ready to be famous?"

"Thank goodness I wore a dress today," she said, kind of joking and kind of not. "Word has already gotten out, even without the interview. People are calling from hours away and asking me to work with their dogs.

The search for Decker was good for business. I just wish that we knew something solid about what happened to him." She paused. "Texas Law has installed a state-of-the-art security system at my house, with cameras and alarms and direct dial to emergency services. Still, it makes me nervous to be alone. Well, me and Gypsum."

"Starting tonight, I'll be with you." Bruce pushed up from where he was sitting on the side of the bed. After more than a week of rest, his legs were heavy. Still, he walked to where Hannah stood and reached for her hand. He laced his fingers through hers, until they were connected. A single unit.

"The guest room is all ready for you. Shana told me all your favorite foods. The kitchen is stocked. You'll be well cared for," she said, giving his hand a squeeze.

He had no doubt that he was going to be just fine at Hannah's place. And sure, he knew that he was going to be sleeping in the guest room. It's just that he wanted more from her—romantically and physically. Those few kisses on the trail had awakened something in Bruce that he'd thought had died all those years ago. Before he could say anything, there was a knock on the door. Without waiting for a reply, Ryan stepped inside.

Hannah and Bruce continued to hold hands. If Ryan had an opinion about their burgeoning romance, he kept it to himself. "They're setting up a table with microphones downstairs. An orderly will be by with a wheelchair to get you, Bruce. The doctor said you can't talk for more than five minutes. Speaking to the media should be pretty painless—or so I hope."

An orderly—a young, blonde woman—entered the

room. "Knock, knock. I heard we have a celebrity who needs limo service."

It was a bit of a cheesy joke, but Bruce laughed. "I've never ridden in a limo—or a wheelchair for that matter."

He gave Hannah's hand a final squeeze. Then he let her go and settled into the seat. Bruce wore sneakers and rested his feet on the footplates. He was backed out of the room before being wheeled down the hall. Hannah and Ryan followed. The elevator was waiting, and it took only a few seconds for them to descend to the ground floor.

There were no other sounds beyond the squeaking of rubber-soled shoes on the tiled floor. As they drew closer to the conference room, he could hear a buzz of conversation. Bruce couldn't help but wonder, *What have I agreed to do?*

Hannah walked into the conference room and stumbled to a stop. When she'd agreed to speak at a press conference, she hadn't been exactly sure what she'd envisioned. Maybe she'd thought it would just be a few local reporters who would use their cell phones to capture videos that would later be posted to the internet. But that had been a naive assumption.

A single table sat at the back of the room. Behind the table were three chairs. The small conference room was filled with a forest of cameras. She recognized one of the reporters from a Dallas TV station. Hell, there was even a media personality from a national cable network, as well as a cadre of other reporters from markets all over southern Texas.

The orderly wheeled Bruce up to the table. Hannah took a seat at his side. Ryan sat in a chair beside hers. A group of microphones was huddled together in the middle of the table, right in front of Hannah.

The reporter from Dallas stood up and raised her hand. "I'm Rita Martinez. KDLS. Can you each say and spell your name for the record?"

Both men looked at Hannah. Without either of them saying a word, she knew that she was to go first. A thousand butterflies let loose in her middle. She swallowed down her nerves. Leaning into the microphones, she said, "I'm Hannah Jefferies." Then she spelled her name.

Bruce and Ryan each did the same.

The reporter from Dallas was still standing. "Bruce, we heard that you were shot by the infamous killer Decker Newcombe. How are you feeling now?"

"Well, I'm being released as soon as I talk to you all. So, I guess I'm doing okay." The reporters nodded, smiled, and a few chuckled. "Really," he continued, "I'm lucky to be here. Hannah saved my life. She gave me first aid until Ryan and all the other folks from Texas Law arrived. They had enough foresight to bring a nurse with them. Then, I got good care at this hospital."

Rita asked another question. "How was it that you ended up in a gunfight with Decker?"

The memories of those few minutes always lived at the edge of Hannah's thoughts. She tried not to dwell on what had happened. During the day, it was easier to keep away the dark thoughts. But in the dark, she relived the nightmare, even when she was awake.

"Decker only wanted the vehicle we had. I'm not surprised that he was desperate to get out of the desert, but he killed three other good men trying to get the keys. Hannah shot the killer and then he and I wrestled for his gun. I ended up on the losing end of that wrestling match."

Another reporter stood up. He held a cellular phone. "I'm Evan Watson from the *San Antonio Examiner.*" Hannah was familiar with the popular newspaper. In her opinion, they were the best at covering anything that happened in the Texas statehouse. "Hannah, as Bruce mentioned, you shot Decker Newcombe. Any idea where he was wounded?"

She leaned toward the group of microphones. "From what I could tell from where he bled, I think he was hit in the abdomen or the side."

"Is it true that an abdominal injury is usually fatal?"

"I'm not a doctor," she said. "So, I can't answer that question."

Evan raised his hand. "Are there any updates on Decker's whereabouts?"

Ryan said, "Texas Law is working with all our law enforcement partners. It's an all-hands-on-deck kind of moment. But so far, we haven't gotten any credible leads. I want to remind everyone that if you think you've seen Decker Newcombe, contact your local police or the FBI. Decker is considered armed and dangerous." He paused. "But mark my words, we've cut off his lifelines. There is nobody else out there to help him. It's only a matter of time before he's caught."

Hannah was buoyed by Ryan's words. She hoped he was right. Yet she knew firsthand that with Decker, nobody should be too confident.

Chapter 15

Decker Newcombe sat in the corner of a bar outside of Rio Bravo, Mexico. He wore a baseball cap that was pulled low over his brow and a pair of sunglasses. It wasn't the best disguise but, so far, he hadn't been arrested. He was certain that the SUV he had stolen and later ditched had been recovered. It meant that the Mexican National Guard knew he was in the country. Even now, the local police were likely out looking for him.

But for more than a week, he'd moved through the border communities like a ghost.

Once he'd gotten into Mexico, he'd traded one of the guns he'd stolen from a Texas Law operative for medical care. The wound to his side and upper arm still ached, but he'd survived. He'd also sold the semiautomatic rifle and had gotten enough cash to keep him fed.

A TV hung on the wall above a long mahogany bar and several neon signs for locally brewed cervezas. He picked up his bottle of orange soda and took a sip. His gaze was captured by the image on the screen. A dark-haired woman stood in front of the small hospital in Encantador—a place he had seen more than once. The chyron at the bottom of the screen read "KDLS Crime

Reporter, Rita Martinez." Setting his bottle on the table, he leaned forward so he could hear what the TV reporter said.

"Today, I'm in a small town near the southern border that has been devastated by the serial killer Decker Newcombe. Since he's been on the run in Wyoming, through Texas, until now, Decker has been responsible to for multiple deaths of innocent people. For the towns of Encantador and neighboring Mercy, all the killings have become personal. Local private security firm, Texas Law, was hired to assist in tracking Decker down. Last week, after Newcombe killed three members of a group of campers, Texas Law sent in group of operatives to find and apprehend the killer. As many of you may remember, three employees from Texas Law have died and one other person—a local guide—was shot by Newcombe.

"That injured man, Bruce McDaniel, was released from the hospital earlier today. I was at that press conference, and you can see what was said."

The image on the screen changed to a conference table with three people sitting in a row. He knew them all. There was Hannah—the woman with the dog. Bruce—the man he'd shot. And Ryan Steele—his onetime friend and now his worst enemy.

The bartender, an older woman with streaks of gray in her dark hair, lifted a remote from behind a counter and pointed it at the TV.

"Don't change that channel," said Decker, his voice coming out with more force than he had intended.

There was only a handful of people in the establishment, and they all turned to him and stared. *So much for keeping a low profile.* Then again, he didn't care that he'd been noticed—not if it meant getting information on the investigation.

After a moment, the bartender shrugged and set the remote down.

Ryan was talking, speaking directly into the camera. "Decker is considered armed and dangerous." He paused. "But mark my words, we've cut off his lifelines. There is nobody else out there to help him. It's only a matter of time before he's caught."

Decker's pulse spiked, the wounds in his arm and side throbbing with each beat of his heart. How was he stuck in some Podunk bar in Nowheresville, Mexico, while Ryan was being interviewed? White-hot anger filled his belly until lava flowed through his veins.

He'd quit listening to the reporter or anything else from the press conference. If he'd been more attentive, he would have noticed the instant his picture was flashed onto the screen. Along with the photo was a phone number to call in case Decker was sighted. The reporter ended her segment by saying, "There's a reward being offered for information that leads to the apprehension of Decker Newcombe." She repeated the phone number. "Back to you in the studio."

One of the patrons glanced over his shoulder. Then the man faced forward and leaned into his friend, whispering something that Decker couldn't hear. Then again, he knew what was being said. *That's the guy from the TV. I'm sure that's the serial killer and if we turn him in now, we'll get the reward money.*

Decker's first instinct was to kill both patrons. After all, dead men can't contact the National Guard. But he didn't have time. He rose from his seat and walked briskly out the door. As he stepped onto the bright street, he shoved his hands in his pockets and walked to the corner.

A new thought came to him with each step. He was a descendant of Jack the Ripper. It didn't matter that all his contacts were gone—either dead or in jail. He was destined for greatness. He could still fulfill his dream of becoming the most famous killer of all time. And now, he knew exactly what he had to do.

After the press conference wrapped up, Hannah left the hospital through a side door to avoid any more media. A white sun hung in a sky of soft blue. Waves of heat undulated over the parking lot. Her SUV was parked in a spot near the door. From ten paces away, she used the fob to unlock the door and start the engine.

After opening the door, she waited a moment for the interior to cool. Sliding into the driver's seat, she put the gearshift into Drive and made her way to the same side exit she had used moments before. Pulling up to the curb, she parked her vehicle and waited.

The door opened. One orderly held the door while another pushed Bruce through in a wheelchair. Hannah got out and stepped onto the asphalt. Heat seeped through the soles of her shoes and the inside of her nose burned with each breath.

"Omigosh," she gushed. "Is that really Bruce McDaniel? I saw him on the news."

Bruce chuckled. "Very funny, especially since you're going to be on the TV with me."

She opened the passenger door. "Let's get you out of here before someone asks for an autograph."

Using the strength of his good arm, Bruce pushed himself out of the seat. He moved stiffly but, still, he was standing. That had to count for something. Walking slowly, he climbed into the passenger seat. Hannah gave him a quick smile and pushed the door shut.

"These are his orders," the orderly said, handing her a stack of papers. "As well as information for his first in-home PT visit."

"I'll make sure he follows all the directions." Then she rounded to the driver's side and got behind the wheel. After shifting into Drive, she waved at the orderly and pulled away from the curb.

"How are you feeling?"

A stop sign stood at the edge of the parking lot. She stepped on the brake and the car rolled to a stop.

"Happy to be out of the hospital."

"I bet." Hannah checked the intersection. There was no traffic, and she pulled onto the road. For several minutes, the miles slipped away. Bruce was quiet and she figured he deserved a little silence. Soon the town of Encantador was just a speck in the rearview mirror.

Adjusting her grip on the wheel, she steered with one hand and glanced at Bruce. In the passenger seat, his chin resting in his palm, he was looking out the window.

Energy—excitement and nervousness both—buzzed through her veins. It left her jittery and the silence became an oppressive force. "Penny for your thoughts," she said.

Bruce glanced in her direction and smiled. "I'd have to give you a refund. I wasn't thinking of anything." He paused. "Or nothing much, really."

"Oh?"

He looked back out the window. "I was just thinking about how pretty it is around here. I know this area isn't for everyone. It's hot. It's dry. Not a lot of commerce and even less of a population. But for me, it's home, and I'm just thankful to be alive."

"That sounds pretty profound to me."

He looked at her again and reached for her hand. "Thanks for everything. You've done a hell of a job taking care of me."

She let him lace his fingers through hers. Holding Bruce's hand was nice. Knowing that he'd be staying with her for the next several weeks was nicer. Still, since their stolen kisses in the tent, they'd been completely platonic—the occasional hand-holding notwithstanding. She squeezed his palm. "What'd you think of the press conference?"

"I'm glad I don't have to do those every day. I was careful about everything I said, and worried about making an ass out of myself." He hesitated before asking, "How 'bout you? What'd you think?"

"About the same." Only minutes ago, she'd hated the silence. Now, she couldn't think of anything else to say.

"Is Shana waiting for me at your house?"

"Last I heard, she was on her way over. So she should be there by the time we get back." She turned onto the road where she lived. "Your daughter insisted on making a week's worth of dinners. She told me that there's chicken noodle soup and homemade bread waiting for you. I made an apple pie before I left. We'll have a little party to celebrate that you were released from the hospital."

"So long as there are no reporters," he joked.

"No reporters," she said. "I promise."

She turned onto her driveway. The old farmhouse stood on a rise. The windows winked with reflected sunlight. With her newest clients, she'd be able to pay a professional to paint the whole house. If she were lucky, she'd have enough left over to fix the porch and build the kennel that she wanted.

Gypsum stood on the porch. The dog barked and wagged her tail.

Sure, Hannah hadn't lived in Mercy for long. But as she parked her vehicle next to the house, she finally felt like she was home.

After turning off the ignition, she got out but stopped in her tracks as a wave of heat slapped her in the face. Bruce opened the passenger door.

Shana stepped onto the porch and the screen door swung shut with a slam.

Hannah tensed. It wasn't like her to be jumpy. But in the back of her mind, she heard a gun's report. She saw Trey's severed head, lying on the ground.

She shook away the memories and smiled at Bruce's daughter.

Shana's blond hair was tied back into a ponytail, and

she wore scrubs with cartoon cats on the shirt. Smiling wide, she waved. "Dad! You're here."

Bruce stepped down from the vehicle. "Hey, honey," he said, spreading his arms for a hug. "It's good to see you."

Shana rushed toward her father. "Seeing you at the hospital reminded me of Mom. I was so worried that you wouldn't make it..."

Hannah stood next to the driver's door as indecision weighed her down. She wasn't sure what to do with herself. After all, this was a moment for father and daughter. She was just a friend, and a new one at that.

Then Gypsum ran off the porch and came to Hannah. Kneeling, she buried her face in the dog's fur. "Hey, girl," she whispered. "I'm home."

Gypsum licked the side of her face. After hugging the dog once more, Hannah stood and shook out her skirt. In taking a knee, she'd gotten dirt on her dress. It was one of the many reasons she liked jeans best.

Shana and Bruce came to her side of the SUV. "Come on in," said Shana. "I made myself at home—like you said—and have everything out for lunch."

Bruce pressed his hand to his stomach. "Homemade bread, soup and pie. Sounds more like a feast to me."

"I'll get your bag," said Hannah while opening the rear liftgate.

"I'm being cooked for and having my bag carried. I can get used to all this special treatment. Maybe I ought to get shot more often," said Bruce.

It was obvious by his words and tone that he was joking. Still, she groaned. "Please don't."

Shana had filled a large duffel bag with Bruce's clothes and toiletries, which she'd had delivered to the hospital during the early days of his recovery. It was that same bag that Hannah removed from the back of her SUV now. With Gypsum at her side, she climbed the porch steps. Bruce and Shana followed.

She walked through the front door. The air conditioner was on, leaving the house pleasantly cool. The yeasty scent of freshly baked bread mixed with the salty and savory smell of chicken soup. Through it all was the sweet and spicy aroma from the apple pie. Her stomach grumbled with hunger. Pressing her hand to her middle, she said, "Smells delicious."

In the kitchen, Shana had set three places at the table. A pot of soup sat on a trivet and a loaf of bread was sliced and in a basket. There were also three glasses filled with iced tea. Shana had placed a bouquet of flowers in a vase, and it sat on the middle of the table.

"Thanks for setting everything up," said Hannah, squeezing Shana's shoulder in for a side hug. "It all looks great and smells delicious."

"This is the least I can do," she said, pulling out a chair. "You've been so great to help my dad through all of this. The flowers are a gift from me, by the way. Sit. Let's eat while it's hot."

Hannah took a seat opposite Shana. Bruce sat between them. "Well, I owe you both so much." He raised his glass of tea. "Here's to you both. My two favorite women."

She sipped her tea and assumed that Bruce was just being kind by including her in the same league as his daughter. Certainly, they'd become closer over the past week. They had bonded during the nightmarish two days with the search party. As the only two who'd survived, it made them some kind of kin. But what if it wasn't just platitudes? Was there something more between them than just friendship?

It was impossible to forget the fact that they'd kissed. But had that desire been real or just a reaction to their dangerous situation? Hannah was old enough to know that sometimes a kiss didn't mean much.

"Hand me your bowl," said Shana. "I'll serve the soup."

Hannah took another sip of tea and set her glass on the table before passing her bowl. She waited as Shana ladled in savory broth that was filled with carrots, celery, wide noodles and chunks of chicken. Bruce handed the dish back to Hannah and then he held out the basket of bread. She took a slice, along with a smear of butter from the crock.

For several minutes, the only sound was the clinking of spoons against bowls. As Bruce sopped up broth with his slice of bread, he said, "You know the food is good when all conversation stops."

"In this case, you're right. The soup tastes as good as it looks." Hannah took her last bite of bread and pushed her bowl away. Rising, she said, "I have pie. Who wants a slice?"

"I'll take one," said Shana. Whatever she was going to say next was interrupted by the ringing of a phone. She pulled her cell from a pocket in her scrubs. After glancing at the screen, Shana frowned. "Hold on a minute. This call is from my office." Swiping the call open, she got up from her seat. Walking out of the kitchen, she said, "Hey, Kyle. What's up?"

Hannah was still on her feet. "What about you? You ready for a slice of pie?"

"Sure," said Bruce. He stood, as well. "I can clear the table."

She waved away his offer to help. "Just relax. You've been through a lot. I can clean up the kitchen once you're settled."

"I insist," he said, picking up his bowl and stacking it inside hers.

"Really," she said, "just relax." Hannah reached for the dishes. Her fingertips brushed the back of his hand. An electric charge shot up her arm and left her heart racing. She raised her eyes and met his gaze. His pulse thrummed at the base of his neck.

He leaned forward, coming close enough that she could feel the whisper of his breath on her cheek. Her mouth tingled with the memory of his lips on hers. She wanted him closer. To feel the heat of his skin and how he was solid and male.

"Well." Shana's voice came from the hallway. Bruce stepped back quickly, still holding the bowls. "That was my assistant. He said there's an emergency, so I have to go. I wasn't planning on working this afternoon, but I know that you'll get settled here, Dad. Is it okay if I call you this evening and check in?"

Hannah's face grew hot. Had Shana seen anything? God, how embarrassing to get caught by Bruce's daughter. A flush crept up her chest. Lifting a cloth napkin from the table, she fanned herself.

"Are you okay?" Shana placed her hand on Hannah's shoulder.

"Just a hot flash," she lied, setting the napkin back on the table. "Do you want to take a slice of pie with you?"

"I do, but I don't have time," she said, pulling her father in for a quick hug. "Take care of yourself and I love you."

"I love you, too," Bruce called out as Shana strode down the hallway.

The front door opened and closed. From outside came the sounds of a car engine starting and the crunch of tires over gravel as the vehicle drove away.

As the sounds of the car faded into nothing, Hannah could hear the racing of her pulse. She was keenly aware that she and Bruce were alone. There was nobody to interrupt. What would happen now?

Chapter 16

Hannah took the dishes from Bruce. "I'll get these cleaned and then we can have some dessert."

She walked to the sink and rinsed the bowls and spoons before placing them in the dishwasher.

Standing next to the counter, Bruce held the basket filled with bread and the final bowl from the table. "What do you want me to do with these?"

"Set the bowl in the sink," she said. "I'll get a container for the bread."

She took a step back as he stepped forward. Hannah bumped into his hips with her rear. He steadied her with a hand on her waist.

"Are you okay?" he asked, his words washing over her shoulder.

"I'm fine." She was better than fine. A delicious feeling unraveled in her middle. Hannah turned to face him. Bruce still held the bowl and basket in one hand. The other hand was on her waist. "I got those," she said, taking the dishes from his grasp. Without looking at him, she placed everything on the counter. "Are you ready for dessert?"

He leaned against the counter. "I want whatever you want."

The double entendre was obvious.

But he was a guest in her home. He was there because he needed help. Over the past week, they'd become friends. What would happen if they made love and things got awkward?

Turning on the taps, she rinsed the last bowl and placed it on the rack with the other dishes. Then she put the remaining bread into a container with a lid and left it on the counter. Her movements were rote, like she'd been put on to an automatic setting. Bruce stood at her side and watched as she worked.

She glanced at him from her periphery. "What?"

He smiled. "I just like watching you, is all."

"Watching me?" she joked. "You must really be bored."

"You have to know that you're beautiful."

Oh sure, Hannah knew that she was attractive. But beautiful? "Hardly."

"Guys in Dallas must've been lined up around the block to go out with you."

Over the years, Hannah had learned to care less, after being let down by the dating scene in Dallas. Men who seemed to go after women who were artificially enhanced or wore tons of makeup, or the latest fashions… not women like her, who spent time in jeans and T-shirts, covered in dog hair. She tried to embrace who she was as a person. But the compliment still fell flat with her—just like hearing an out-of-tune piano.

She leaned her hip on the counter. "I'm not the kind

of woman who guys line up to take out." He opened his mouth. Before he could argue, she continued. "I'm fine with that—really, I am. So, you don't have to flatter me."

"It's not flattery if it's true. You are beautiful. I love the way your hair turns red and gold in the sunlight. I love that you have flecks of green in your eyes. I love that you have a crease in your lip." He touched his own mouth. "Right there."

She wasn't one for staring at her reflection in the mirror. But in Bruce's eyes, she did feel beautiful. "Thank you for that."

He shifted, moving closer to her. She could kiss him, if she wanted. Just pull him to her and place her mouth on his. They were adults and they had the whole afternoon to themselves. But she was meant to be caring for him. If Bruce wasn't supposed to stay by himself, he certainly wasn't healthy enough for sex. "I should get the soup into the fridge before it goes bad."

She moved to the table. Bruce caught her hand, stopping her. "The soup will keep. Stay with me for a minute."

She could tell him, *No*. But he wanted her. And she liked being desired. "Well," she said, moving to him, "you have me. Now, what do you want to do?"

He placed his hand on her cheek and looked into her eyes. For the first time in years, Hannah felt admired, cherished, and seen. It was an intoxicating mix and left her lightheaded. "What do I want?" he asked, repeating her question. "I want to do this."

He placed his mouth on hers. His kiss tasted of fresh bread and sweet iced tea. She wrapped her arms around his neck, pulling him closer. His tongue pressed on the seam of her lips. She sighed, letting him slip his tongue into her mouth.

Bruce pressed her back until her butt was against the counter. She pulled him closer. She could feel his hardness, straining against the fabric of his jeans. She rocked her hips forward, pressing into him.

"Oh, Hannah," he groaned.

She ran her fingers through his hair as he blazed a trail of kisses from her mouth to her cheek to her neck. His hands moved from her waist to the front of her stomach. His touch inched upward, leaving gooseflesh in its wake. He cupped one of her breasts, and she wanted more.

She claimed his mouth with her own, kissing him deeply, hungrily, as if she'd never been kissed before and might not be kissed again. In a way, that was true. With Bruce, everything was new and soft and sincere. But there was a decidedly carnal edge to their embrace. He stroked his thumb across her areola. Even through the fabric of her dress, her nipple hardened.

He pulled at the neck of her dress and the cup of her bra, freeing her breast. He bent his head to her, flicking his tongue over her nipple. Then he moved to her other breast. She gripped the back of his head, pulling him closer.

"Bruce," she said, breathing the word into his hair.

He kissed her again and reached for the hem of her dress. He pulled it up, gathering fistfuls of fabric. The cool air kissed her ankles. Her calves. Her thighs. With a finger, he stroked the waist of her panties. The anticipation of his touch left her giddy. Then he slid his hand inside her underwear. He traced a line down the front of her sex. She was already wet and weak with want. He slid a finger inside Hannah. Her muscles clenched around him as the friction of his touch built. It felt like a fire burned in her veins and she was about to be consumed by the inferno.

"I want you," he said, kissing her again.

Hannah wanted Bruce, too. Here. Now. It didn't matter that they were in the kitchen. "Are you sure that you're well enough to do this?"

"I'm positive," he said, gripping her side.

Hannah wanted him more with a desire that bordered on pain.

"I have a condom." The likelihood of getting pregnant during perimenopause was slim. But she wasn't willing to take that risk. Now, where had she put the box? Her eye was drawn to a single box that sat in the corner of the kitchen. It was with all the odds and ends that she hadn't yet needed and therefore hadn't yet put away.

"Hold on." She let her dress fall back into place as she walked quickly to the packing carton. She unfolded the lid flaps. There on top was a black box. She took out a single foil packet. "Here you go," she said, handing it to Bruce.

He took it and paused a moment. Had he changed his mind? Should she suggest they go to her bedroom? "It's been years since I've done this," he said. "I'm glad that my first time is with you."

Before she could say anything, he kissed her hard, pressing against her as she backed up. She was pinned between Bruce and the cabinets. Hannah lifted herself onto the counter and let her knees fall open. Bruce unzipped the fly of his jeans and rolled the condom down his length. She pulled up the hem of her dress as he moved aside her panties. He entered her slowly, inch by inch.

She wasn't as wet as she thought. She was tighter, too. The combination made her thankful that he was taking it slow. Then he was inside her all the way. He began pumping his hips and they fell into a rhythm. He rubbed the top of her sex, and she felt her climax began to build.

She cried out as she came. Bruce drove into her harder and faster. With a low growl, he came, as well. As he kissed her softly, Hannah still didn't believe in forever kind of love, but she was happy with her life for now.

Hannah was standing in the middle of the desert. Storm clouds roiled overhead, blotting out the moonlight. A shadowy figure moved in the darkness. It was Decker. Her feet turned icy cold and her hands started to shiver. She should run, but she was too terrified to move or scream.

As Decker walked toward her, she could see that he carried something in his hand.

Then she saw Trey's severed head. Blood dripped from where his neck had once been. His eyes stared at nothing, and his mouth was opened in a silent scream.

Sitting up, she clutched the sheet to her chin. The room was still dark, but she recognized her own bed. There was the outline of her dresser against one wall, and the window, covered with sheers, on the other side of the room. A thin sheen of sweat coated her brow and clung to her chest. She used the sheet to wipe her damp face.

"What's the matter?" Bruce lay on the pillow next to hers. He reached for her hand and Hannah let go of the covers. She laced her fingers through his. "Bad dream, again?"

Since being released from the hospital three days before, Bruce hadn't spent a single night in the guest room. Instead, he'd moved into Hannah's bedroom and slept with her. That's when the nightmares began. The first night, she'd assumed that it was just delayed reaction to the trauma she'd experienced at the hands of Decker Newcombe. But as the same bad dream came to her for the third time, she wondered if there was more.

Her racing pulse returned to normal and she lay back on the pillow. Snuggling under the blankets, she said, "I'm sorry I woke you."

Bruce pulled her to him, shifting them both so that her back rested against his chest. "Don't apologize. I'm here for you now. Always."

"I'm glad you're with me." Bruce's mention of forever left Hannah feeling like the walls were closing in from all sides. At first, she'd been worried about his feelings—not hers. But she'd been married twice already. Was she ready for that kind of commitment now? Or ever? She ran her fingertips over his arm, tracing the cords of muscles. "Go back to sleep."

"You need your rest, too." He paused. "Do you think that you should talk to someone? Like a professional therapist or a counselor? They could help you navigate all your feelings and fears about what happened."

"I tried counseling before my first divorce. It didn't work."

"Marriage counseling is a whole lot different than what you'd talk about now."

He was probably right. Still, Hannah wasn't ready to go to a therapist just yet. "I'll think about it."

"I just want what's best for you."

She lifted his hand to her lips and kissed his knuckles. "I know."

Hannah wasn't used to a man who wanted to take care of her. And she understood that Bruce's caring was part of the reason she felt claustrophobic. It was unreasonable on her part, she knew, especially since she liked being around him. He was funny. Kind. Smart. Brave.

But still she worried that there was something she was missing. After all, both of her husbands had seemed great in the beginning. By the time she'd realized that they'd had serious character flaws, it was too late.

Or was she the problem? Was Hannah somehow unlovable?

Bruce kissed the back of her neck. The feeling of his lips on her flesh drew her out of her thoughts.

She hummed in satisfaction as goose bumps rose on her arms. "That feels nice."

"You like that?" He lifted her hair at the nape and kissed her again. "What about this?" Another kiss. "Or this."

She snuggled deeper into his embrace. "I like it all."

"What about this?" He reached around to touch her

breasts. Through the thin fabric of her sleep shirt, he rolled her nipple between his finger and thumb.

Instinctively, she arched her back, pressing her breast into his hand. Her hips rocked into his pelvis. Bruce was already hard. A tingling sensation danced along her skin. She wanted him inside her just as much as he wanted her. Even if she had misgivings about forever, she could still enjoy the now. She rubbed her butt against him.

"You're driving me crazy," he said, nipping her earlobe.

"That's kind of the idea."

He reached between her legs and ran his fingers down the inside of her panties. He found the top of her sex. She was wet and swollen with want. He began to rub, and the tingling turned into an electric current that pulsed through Hannah. She could feel her orgasm begin to build from his first touch. Every cell in her body was like a live wire. The energy surged through her veins until she had no choice but to give in to the sensation.

"Bruce," she cried out as she came. "Bruce. Bruce."

It was funny how after just a few nights together, he knew her body better than anyone had before. And maybe ever would again. She lay on her back and slipped out of her panties. As Bruce took off his boxer shorts, she opened the drawer of her nightstand and found the box of condoms. She removed a single packet and handed it to Bruce. He rolled the rubber down his hard length as she settled onto the mattress and let her legs fall open.

He entered her slowly and they fell into a rhythm. Hannah wrapped her legs around his waist, and he thrust inside her deeper and harder. She gripped his ass. The feeling of his muscles moving was hypnotic.

Bruce reached for one hand and then the other. He pressed her wrists onto the bed. "You're mine." Even in the dark, she could see his eyes.

She was trapped, but in truth, Hannah didn't want to get away. "I'm yours," she said. "Yours and nobody else's."

His breath came in short and ragged gasps as he drove into her hard. And harder still. He closed his eyes and moaned as he came. Spent, Bruce flopped on top of Hannah. She unwound her legs from his waist. For a moment, the two of them lay, sharing a breath and heart-beat. Bruce pressed his palm against hers. He kissed her again, softly this time. "You are mine," he said. "But I have to take care of the condom."

He rose, slipping out from inside her, and padded softly across her bedroom floor to the bathroom across the hallway. Hannah took a moment to find her discarded skivvies and put them back on. As she settled into the pillow, Bruce returned. He redressed and slid under the covers.

With Bruce on his back and Hannah's head on his chest, she let his heartbeat lull her toward sleep.

"What do you think about that?" The rumble of Bruce's voice pulled Hannah from the edge of slumber.

"What do I think about *what*?"

"About you being mine and nobody else's."

Hannah understood that what Bruce had said was more than sexy talk, even when she agreed. She also knew that she didn't want to have this conversation right now. But to avoid the topic would be dishonest.

Pushing onto her elbow, she said, "I like you, Bruce. I like you a lot. I like spending time with you. I like waking up in your arms and making love to you at night. I like watching TV with you. And making dinner together. And I like knowing that you are in the house while I'm working. But—"

"But?" he interrupted.

"But this relationship is new. To be honest, I thought that you were still in love with your wife."

"I am. I was." Bruce let out a long breath. "For too long, I was tied up by my grief. It was like finding you loosened all those knots. I don't know how to describe it, other than to tell you that I know what I want from life—and it's to be with you."

"To me, your change feels sudden. It makes me wonder if I'm just a new toy for you to play with and, eventually, you'll get tired of me." She didn't add that she also worried that Bruce would discover that she was broken or somehow unlovable.

"I don't see you as a toy and I'm not playing games..."

"But do you understand my point?"

He let out a long breath. "Yeah. I get it."

"Remember all those things I said about how much I like you?" She didn't wait for an answer. "They're all still true. But I'd like to slow things down a bit, especially when it comes to talking about a long-term future. When we first met, I wasn't looking for another relationship. Two failed marriages had soured me on love. But you're different and I want to be with you. But I'm not sure I'm the type of person who is meant for forever." She hadn't meant to be so honest. But she couldn't take back her words now. "Is that enough?"

Bruce placed his lips on her forehead. "For you, I will do anything."

She snuggled back into his arms. This time, when she fell asleep, the nightmare was gone.

Chapter 17

After making love to Hannah, Bruce slept poorly. His body had been sated, but his mind was spinning. He'd known that he'd pushed for more from the relationship than Hannah wanted. But how could he keep staying with her and not want to make their relationship permanent?

Then, there was the problem of Decker Newcombe. Once again, the killer was at-large. Bruce had been determined to catch the killer, and he'd failed. Three more men had died, and he was just lucky to be alive. Too many times, people had thought the killer would move on and leave the town of Mercy alone.

But he kept coming back.

If Bruce were a betting man, he'd place money on Decker's return. But when and where?

Well, that was anyone's guess.

After hours of tossing and turning, he still hadn't answered that question.

Shades had been pulled over the window. But soft light shone around the edges. It was dawn—or close to it—and he slid quietly from the bed. Gypsum had settled on the foot of the mattress, and she jumped to the floor as he walked quietly out of the room. The dog followed, her nails clicking on the floorboards.

Bruce might be sharing a bed with Hannah, but his belongings were still stowed in the guest room. He found a pair of jeans and a T-shirt and dressed quickly. With the dog at his side, he descended the stairs and made his way to the kitchen. Sunlight streamed through a window over the sink. The rays reflected off the white counters and the chrome appliances until the room seemed to glow.

The first two mornings at Hannah's house, she'd made him breakfast. But Bruce had been single for more than seven years and could fend for himself. He opened the refrigerator and scanned the contents. There was bacon, eggs, wheat bread, real butter and orange juice. It was all the things he liked to eat. After pulling out everything from the fridge, he set it on the counter.

Gypsum lay on the floor, watching him.

"Any idea where she keeps the frying pan?" he asked.

The dog yawned and lay down, resting her head on her paws. "You're a good search dog, but you aren't much help in the kitchen."

Bruce opened several cabinets before finding one with cookware. He removed the frying pan and set it on the stove, before turning on the burner to medium-high. Once the pan was hot, he laid several strips of bacon across the bottom. They began to sizzle, and the room filled with a salty scent.

Preparing a meal kept his hands busy, but it didn't keep his mind from wandering. He'd fallen for Hannah, and hard. He knew that he didn't view her as a toy—

something to be played with and discarded when he was bored. But how could he convince her that his feelings were sincere?

"I smell something yummy," said Hannah, walking into the kitchen. She'd pulled her hair into a ponytail, donned a red robe, and wore flip-flops. In his opinion, she looked amazing.

"I wanted to let you sleep a little extra and make breakfast for you." He flipped the bacon over. "How do you like your eggs?"

"I'll take them any way you want to cook them," she said. "Having someone make me a meal is a treat."

Hannah opened a cabinet and removed a bag of coffee. She put several scoops into a paper filter and started the coffee machine. Instantly, the nutty smell of coffee mixed with the aroma of the bacon. "If heaven has a scent, this might be it," he said.

"If heaven is filled with breakfast food, you can sign me up," she said.

"You want to start some toast?" he asked. "The bacon's almost ready and it won't take long to scramble the eggs."

"I can make that." She put four slices of bread into a slotted toaster and then removed two plates, mugs and juice glasses from the cupboard. "I'll be back in a minute. I need to take Gypsum outside."

While she was gone, Bruce plated the bacon and scrambled several eggs.

As he was dividing the eggs onto two plates, Hannah and Gypsum returned.

"It smells great in here," she said, retrieving a dog

dish and bag of kibble from a pantry tucked into a corner near the stove. "You're a rare man, Bruce McDaniel. Handsome. Brave. Hardworking. And a hell of a cook."

Her compliment confused him more than before. If he was all those things, why was Hannah reluctant to commit to a relationship?

As she filled the dog dish, the bread popped up from the toaster, warm and golden brown.

"Looks like everything's ready," said Bruce, putting two slices of bread on each plate with the eggs. He added strips of bacon.

Hannah filled mugs with coffee and glasses with orange juice. She placed both on the table as he set down the plates. The ceramic hit the wooden table with a *clink.*

Hannah sucked in a quick breath as the color in her face paled.

"You okay?" he asked, sliding into a chair.

"I'm fine," she said, picking up a glass of juice. Her hand trembled and juice sloshed over the rim. "Just a little jumpy this morning."

"Is something bothering you?" Was it him? Suddenly, Bruce wasn't hungry anymore.

"Like I mentioned last night, I've been having these dreams," she said. "About what happened, I mean. I keep seeing Trey." She closed her eyes. "Most of the time, I can get through my day, but odd things happen and it brings everything we went through back."

He reached for her, placing his hand on her wrist. "Do you want to talk about it?"

"I should. But just not today."

"I'm here for you."

"I know." She patted the back of his hand and drew her wrist away. Picking up her fork, she scooped up some eggs. Taking the bite, she nodded as she chewed and swallowed. "These are good."

Bruce knew that the conversation was over. He was also learning not to push Hannah. Picking up his own fork, he took a bite of eggs before saying, "Thanks."

"This is a nice way to start the day," she said. "Me. You. Gypsum. Sunshine. Good coffee. Great food."

They ate in silence for a few minutes. Bruce knew he should just enjoy his food, but the eggs sat in his gut like a rock. He couldn't live his life while Hannah always kept him at arm's length. He respected her boundaries, but he wanted things, as well. Didn't he have a right to ask for what he needed and know where things stood?

"I don't get it," he said before deciding if it was wise to say anything at all. "You like me. I like you. Why can't this be a relationship?"

Hannah held a forkful of eggs halfway to her mouth. Sitting taller, she set the cutlery back on the plate with a clink. "Who says this isn't a relationship?"

"You do. You did last night."

She inhaled and exhaled. "I'm not ready to make a commitment to forever, Bruce."

"I know you said that I might change my mind about being with you, but I won't. You just don't know me…"

"Exactly," she said. "What I know about you, I like. But I don't know everything. You had a wonderful life with your wife and, if she hadn't passed away, you would be with her still."

Hannah was right. Bruce shrugged.

"I'm different. I've walked down the aisle twice and into a divorce attorney's office two times, as well. Marriage hasn't worked out for me the way it worked out for you. I don't want to make that same mistake again, so I'm going to take my time before committing to anyone. But it doesn't mean that I'm not excited to be with you right now."

Bruce wasn't sure what to say next. Taking a bite of eggs, he gave himself time to think. "Where does that leave us? Do you want me to move back to my place?"

Hannah placed her palm on the back of his hand. "I want you here, but only if you want to stay. I'm not rejecting you, Bruce. I'm just asking for time."

Hannah squeezed his hand. "Is that going to work for you?"

The way Bruce saw it, he had two choices. He could leave now and never worry about Hannah again. Or he could slow down his desire to make a lifelong commitment—at least for now. When he thought about it that way, there really was no choice at all. "That'll work for me."

"Good," she said, picking up her fork. Using the tines, she pointed to his plate. "You need to eat. The physical therapist is coming by today."

Bruce liked that someone else knew his schedule and cared. "You're the first good thing to come into my life since Pamela died," he said, letting his hand slip away from hers. "I understand why you want to take things slow, and I think you're right. It's just…"

Hannah swallowed. "It's just what?"

Bruce wasn't sure that he wanted to be completely

candid. Then again, if he wasn't willing to be honest, he was lying to everyone—including himself. "It's just that I'm not going to change my mind about you. About us."

"Then we'll be right for each other later, just like we are now."

He took a sip of coffee and let the caffeine buzz though his system. He had to admit, there was a lot of wisdom in what Hannah said. "So, what are your plans for the day?"

Holding a strip of bacon, she took a bite. "Ryan Steele is coming over for an early morning training session. He has a big surprise planned for the wedding. I'd tell you, but I'm sworn to secrecy."

"Ah, the unbreakable trust between dog trainer and client," he teased.

"Har, har." She gave him a fake laugh. "I gave him my word and I intend to keep it, is all."

Hannah was loyal and honest. Those were two more things to like about her. "What time is he getting here?"

"Seven thirty," she said, popping the rest of her bacon in her mouth. "What time is it?"

There was a digital clock on the microwave's face. "It's seven fifteen already."

"Crap." Hannah stood and grabbed her coffee in one motion. She drank half the cup in a single swallow. "I have to get changed. Don't worry about the dishes. I'll clean up when I get a break."

"I can take care of everything," said Bruce.

"You're supposed to be resting. Recuperating. Besides, you cooked. I should clean. It's only fair."

"I've convalesced more than enough already. Besides,

if I get tired, I can rest. You go. Get ready. Work with Ryan. I've got it all covered."

She took another long drink of coffee before setting the cup on the table. "You're the best," she said and took two steps from the table. Turning around, she grabbed another slice of bacon and piece of toast from her plate. "Don't want the food to go to waste."

Then Hannah placed her lips on the top of his head. "I'll be back once I'm done with Ryan and Old Blue."

He could hear her flip-flops slapping against the floorboards as she walked down the hallway and climbed the stairs. Sitting in the silent kitchen, Bruce took a drink of his coffee. The brew had gone tepid, but he still enjoyed the jolt of caffeine. As he sat, he had to admit that he appreciated his morning with Hannah. She was his equal and she completed him in ways his first wife never had. He understood her reasons for wanting to take their new romance slow and, in theory, he agreed with it all.

But deep in his heart, it felt like playing house. And for Bruce, his feelings for Hannah weren't a game.

Over the next two weeks, Bruce's life settled into a comfortable routine. The day began with him cooking breakfast. Hannah worked with Ryan early every day, and then she came into the house. Over coffee and toast with eggs, they'd talk about their plans.

Bruce's days were always the same. The physical therapist had given exercises meant to help him recover quicker. He did the drills with a fervor that bordered on religious, and he grew stronger every day. The rest of the time, he did paperwork or made calls on behalf of the

Double S Ranch, where he was still the manager. Usually, the business end was handled by the ranch's owner, Sage Sauer. But while he was recovering, he had taken on many of her desk duties. Sage worked with the ranch hands and tended to the cattle—just like Bruce had before his run-in with Decker Newcombe.

Hannah's dog training kept her busy. She had clients coming in every hour. Shana stopped by when she could. If she was seeing patients near Hannah's house, she'd visit for a few minutes or even have lunch with Bruce. Other times, she'd come over after work. One evening, she brought Bruce's truck. Then, he and Hannah drove Shana home.

By suppertime, when Hannah was done with work, she and Bruce would share dinner. After that, they streamed episodes of old sitcoms and finally went to bed. Most nights, they made love before falling asleep. But the thing he loved most of all was holding Hannah throughout the night.

The only problem in his otherwise perfect life was Decker Newcombe. Aside from streaming old TV shows, they watched the news faithfully. Bruce was anxious for news of the killer's whereabouts—and terrified that he'd resurfaced. But as the days passed and he was still at large, Bruce started to worry less. There had been a credible sighting in Rio Bravo, a small town in Mexico, weeks earlier. Since then, nobody had reported seeing Decker at all. Like all those times before, the killer had disappeared. Bruce knew that, eventually, Decker would show up. And when that happened, he had to be ready.

* * *

The day of Kathryn Glass and Ryan Steele's wedding dawned cloudy and cool. For the ceremony, Bruce wore the only suit he owned—a black jacket and trousers, along with a white shirt and blue tie. Standing in front of the bathroom mirror, he straightened the necktie. In the reflection, he saw Hannah walking down the hallway. Her dark hair was pulled up into a twist. A simple strand of pearls hung at her neck. She wore a dress of dark blue that hugged her curves and gave a glimpse of cleavage.

He turned to face her. "You look stunning."

She entered the bathroom and slipped into his arms. She fit next to him perfectly. "You don't look so bad yourself."

Bruce caught their reflection in the mirror. Her hair was dark, where his was light. It was like she was the yin to his yang. A matched set. He kissed her softly. She tasted of minty toothpaste. "We do clean up nicely," he said.

"We do," she agreed while straightening his tie. "Are you ready? We need to leave now so we can get there on time."

Bruce checked his reflection once more before reaching for Hannah's hand and leading her from the bathroom. On the ground floor, Gypsum lay on her bed in Hannah's office. The dog looked up as they walked past, thumping her tail on the floor. He took a detour to pet the dog's head. "You guard the house, girl."

Kissing Gypsum on the snout, she said, "We'll be back soon."

Hannah pulled the front door closed behind her and

twisted the knob to make sure the door was locked. It was. Her SUV was parked next to his truck. She used the fob to unlock her vehicle. After opening the door, she slipped into the driver's seat. He settled into the passenger's seat. Once the doors were closed and the seat belts were secured, she headed down the driveway and turned onto the road leading to Encantador. The ride was unremarkable, and they pulled up in front of the white-clapboard church with fifteen minutes to spare.

The adjacent parking lot was already full. Cars also lined both sides of the street. "Popular event," she remarked while pulling up next to the curb at the end of the block.

Bruce couldn't help it. His hands shook slightly and his stomach twisted into knots. Undoubtedly, the past two weeks with Hannah had been some of the happiest of his life. But he had walked into her house as a friend and now they were lovers. This would be their first time facing the world as a couple.

Walking toward the church, Hannah reached for his hand. Her palm fitted nicely in his. And yet anxiety still twisted in his gut. Bruce had never been the churchgoing type. But all the important events in his life had taken place within the building. It was in this church that he'd married his wife and, a little more than a year later, they had christened baby Shana. The last time he'd been here was for Pamela's funeral.

Crossing the threshold with Hannah at his side was truly taking a step into a new life.

Hannah reached for the crook of his elbow. "Everything okay?"

How was he supposed to explain that she was the sunshine after the rain? That he'd been living in a fog of grief for so long that he worried the light would be blinding? Then again, he needed the warmth of being with Hannah. He placed his palm atop her hand and squeezed gently. "I'm fine. Excellent, really. This place just brings back lots of memories—some good, some not so good." He smiled at Hannah. "But I'm ready to make some new memories with you." He placed his lips on her soft cheek. "You ready?"

"I'm more than ready."

He pulled the door open, holding it as Hannah walked through. The narthex was narrow, with just enough room for a guest book on a stand. Hannah signed her name, and then Bruce signed his. Doors leading to the nave were open. The end of each pew was decorated with a white ribbon and blue flowers. There were flower arrangements at the altar, as well. Behind the pulpit, a harpist played classical music.

Most of the seats were filled. Sage Sauer, his boss, was there with Michael O'Brien. There was Eva Tamke, the nurse who had given him medical care in the desert. She was with her boyfriend, Brett Wilson, the pilot who worked for Texas Law. Issac Patton sat next to his girlfriend, Clare Chamberlain. Theo Fowler, an IT expert who worked for Texas Law, was there. His girlfriend, Ana Pierce and her son, Seth, were also in attendance. Standing at the back of the church were men in dark suits. Bruce figured they were security guards, hired by Texas Law.

He appreciated that everyone understood that Decker

Newcombe was a serious threat. It didn't matter that nobody had seen or heard about killer in weeks. He was out there, somewhere.

Bruce could feel it.

Shana a was already in a pew. She looked over her shoulder and waved. Bruce offered the bend in his elbow to Hannah again and, together, they walked to where his daughter sat. He let Hannah scoot into the seat first, and then he sat next to her.

"You look amazing," said Hannah, giving Shana a quick hug.

She was right, his daughter did look beautiful. Her golden hair, the same color his had been as a younger man, was sleek and gleaming. She wore a dark red dress and shoes to match.

"Hey, honey," he said, reaching across Hannah to squeeze his daughter's hand. "You do look great."

"Well, look at you," she said. "You cleaned up nicely, and you look like you're pretty much healed up. Hannah must be doing a good job taking care of you."

"She's an excellent caretaker."

"Don't let your father lie to you. He's been doing all his PT. He's the one who cooks breakfast and puts something together for lunch."

"Really?" said Shana. With a final squeeze, she let go of his hand. "I'm kind of surprised."

"Why's that? I have been on my own for years. I can cook and clean and take care of myself."

"Yeah, well, as a kid, it seemed like Mom took care of all those chores."

Shana was right. And yet… "I've changed. Improved. Like a fine wine, I'm getting better with age."

Shana laughed and nudged Hannah. "Be honest, are you okay with my dad being in your house? I only thought it was going to be for a few days. But it's been over two weeks and he's still there."

Eventually, they were going to have to have a conversation about him going home. But it wasn't right now, and it definitely wasn't going to be in front of Shana.

Hannah said, "Your dad is really good company." She watched him as she spoke. "I enjoy having him around."

"Well, I have to say, you two looked nice walking down the aisle together."

"Thanks for being subtle, Shana," he said, his tone stern.

A little teasing was all in good fun. But she was a grown woman and should know that there were lines not to be crossed. Like the one insinuating that he should marry Hannah.

"Omigod," said Shana. "I didn't mean it like that… I just think that the two of you look nice together… It's obvious you two like each other and, well, I'm happy for you both. Sorry if I offended anyone."

"I'm not offended," said Hannah. "Really."

"Me, either," said Bruce. He winked at Shana to show that all was forgiven.

The doors at the back of the nave closed and the music fell silent. The wedding was about to begin and despite it all, he really could imagine standing at the altar and watching Hannah walk up the aisle and to him.

Chapter 18

The last chord from the harp floated through the church. It was followed by a pause, just long enough to signal that the ceremony was about to begin. When the music began again—Mendelssohn's "Wedding March" in C major. Everyone rose to their feet—Hannah, included.

Undersheriff Kathryn Glass stood at the rear of the nave, dressed in a creamy white gown with a scooped neckline and sleeves to her elbows. She wore her dark hair pulled into a low bun and carried a bouquet of blue and white flowers. Truly, Kathryn was a lovely bride.

She was accompanied by a teenage boy with Kathryn's coloring.

"That's her son," Shana whispered, "Brock."

It was sweet that the son was walking his mom down the aisle. Even though Hannah didn't know mother or son well, her eyes pricked with tears. She dabbed at her lashes and Bruce reached for her hand. A young woman stood near the altar. She wore a blue dress and had the same features as Brock. Hannah had to guess that the young woman was Kathryn's daughter, and she also guessed that the daughter was serving as the maid of honor.

It was a lovely way to create a new family.

Next, Ryan and the sheriff, Mooky Parsons, came out of the side door. Mooky stood behind the pulpit. Obviously, the sheriff was going to serve as the officiant. Hannah should be paying attention to the ceremony but her mind kept wandering. She thought about the past and how she'd made the decision to walk down the aisle twice before. The first time, she'd been young, in love, and so full of optimism. The second time, she'd grown and changed. She'd felt as if she'd truly understood what commitment looked like. But she'd chosen poorly again.

Shana might not have meant anything when she mentioned that Hannah and Bruce looked good walking down the aisle together. But it left her wondering if the third time really was the charm—or would be for her, at least.

Being with Bruce was wonderful. He was reliable. Strong. Confident but not flashy. He was comfortable, like a cozy sweater on a rainy day.

Then, from the front of the church, Mooky asked, "Do you have the rings?"

Those were the words Hannah had been waiting to hear.

The back door opened and Old Blue, with a blue bow tie at his neck, sauntered into the church. Both wedding bands were attached to the bow. At the altar, Kathryn started to laugh and cry at the same time. "Of course, we couldn't get married without including you. Come here."

Old Blue trotted down the aisle and sat between Kathryn and Ryan.

For the past two weeks, Hannah had been working

with the groom to prepare Old Blue to be the canine ring bearer. It was a surprise for Kathryn and a nice way to include the dog in the service. As Old Blue looked at his people, a doggy smile on his face, she knew that they were going to make a happy family.

As far as Hannah was concerned, the wedding of Ryan Steele and Kathryn Glass had been everything a good wedding should be. The ceremony had been touching and personal. The reception, being held at a restaurant in downtown Encantador, had good food, good drinks, and lots of music for dancing. The dance floor was full as the son of the bride, Brock, did double duty and served as the DJ, as well. Brock played a line dance, the floor thumping with bass. Hannah didn't know the steps, but it didn't stop her from trying.

Bruce stood near the bar, a beer in hand, and spoke to Michael O'Brien. She couldn't hear what the two men discussed. But as she caught Bruce's eye, he lifted his glass before mouthing the word, *Cheers*.

As the song ended, Brock said, "Now, we're going to slow it down. Grab your partner. We want everyone on the floor for this song."

Hannah's hair was damp with sweat. She brushed her bangs off her forehead. At the bar, Bruce drained his beer and set it down. He walked toward her, his hand outstretched. "You heard the man," he said. "We have to dance."

She let him pull her to him. Wrapping her arms around his neck, she swayed to the music. He moved with her, his hands on her hips, like they were made for one another.

"It was a nice wedding," she said, if for no other reason than she needed to make conversation.

"You look like you're having fun," he said, smiling.

God, he really was handsome. "You should be out here with me."

"I can't."

"Because of your injury?"

"Because I can't dance."

"You seem to be doing pretty good right now," she said.

"That's because I'm with you. Everything I do is better when we're together."

That earlier hard knot dropped back into her stomach. Was she ready to try for forever again? Before she could say anything, he placed his lips on hers. The kiss was somehow sweet and passionate at the same time—just like the man who gave it.

She melted against his body, not willing to let go. But not sure that she wanted to stay. The song ended. Bruce pressed his forehead onto hers. "I think I have a new favorite song."

He really was adorable. She needed to decide what was best for her—for him. "Everyone gets romantic at weddings," she said, knowing full well what she was doing. "In a few months, you won't even remember that we danced at all."

Running his hands over her shoulders, he asked, "Is everything okay?"

"Yeah. Of course. I was just trying to be funny. Obviously, I missed the mark." She glanced around the room. Had they stayed at the reception long enough? She opened her mouth, ready to suggest that they head home. Gypsum was a good dog, but she could only stay in the house for so long before needing to be let outside.

Once again, Brock had the microphone. He said, "I'm sure you all know of two wedding traditions—the garter toss and the throwing of a bouquet. I'm sorry to disappoint you single men out there, but we're skipping the garter toss. After all, the bride is my mom." People chuckled. "But I'd like to invite all of the single women to come up here and my mom will toss the bouquet."

Hannah stayed at Bruce's side.

"Oh no. You don't get out of this," Shana said, linking arms with Hannah. "Come with me."

As far as Hannah was concerned, the bouquet toss was for eighteen-year-olds who still believed that marriage was a life plan. Hannah was neither young nor naive. Still, she wasn't going to argue or make a fuss. She was too old and wise to do either of those—especially for something as silly as a bridal bouquet.

More than twenty single women gathered near the DJ table. Hannah stood between Shana and one of the local doctors, a woman named Shelia Garcia. Dr. Garcia rolled her eyes. It might be Hannah's imagination, but she thought that maybe the doctor didn't want to be in the group, either. Then again, if a medical professional could be a good sport, then Hannah could, as well.

The undersheriff stood in front of the room and waved the bouquet in the air. All the women cheered, Hannah included. There was a tickle on the back of her neck. She glanced over her shoulder. At the side of the room, Bruce watched. He'd gotten himself another beer and he lifted the glass in a toast.

She smiled and waved. When she turned forward, a blue-and-white blur was coming straight at her. Her reaction was instinct alone. Reaching out, she caught the bridal bouquet before it hit her in the face.

Hannah didn't need anyone to tell her what catching the wedding flowers meant. The old tradition was too common to miss. She was supposed to be the next person to get married. The only problem was, she wasn't sure if she'd ever want to take that leap again.

Thankfully, Hannah had limited her consumption of alcohol to a single glass of wine with dinner. It meant that when the reception ended, she was stone-cold sober. Bruce had enjoyed himself—and that enjoyment had included several beers.

After the ceremony, they'd driven from the church to the reception hall. The street had been filled with cars at the time, forcing her to park several blocks away and next to the local grocery store. The shop was now closed, the windows dark. As they walked to her SUV, Bruce's eyes were glassy. He swayed slightly, his hip brushing against hers with each step.

"That was a nice wedding," said Bruce. The word came out with extra syllables. *Nii-icce.*

She quietly laughed. "I think you're drunk."

"I'm not drunk. Hell, I only had a few beers all night."

"Okay, you're tipsy then."

"Maybe," he said. "It doesn't mean that the wedding wasn't nice."

The sun had set hours earlier and the night air was cool against her bare skin. Folding her arms across her chest, she tried to conserve body heat as they walked.

"You okay?" he asked, bumping her shoulder.

"Tired. Cold."

He wrapped his arm around her shoulder, pulling her close. "I can warm you up."

The heat from his body wrapped around her. She couldn't help it, and her pulse skipped a beat. Her body craved Bruce's touch. She wanted him next to her—even if she wasn't sure of the next steps in their relationship.

"So," he said before nipping the lobe of her ear. "You caught the bouquet. You know what that means."

"That I need to get out a vase and some water when I get home." She knew she was being both coy and evasive. But, honestly, attending the wedding had stirred up emotions that Hannah had tried her best to forget.

"Har, har."

Hannah said nothing as she unlocked the SUV with the fob.

Her silence did little to stop Bruce. "I'd like to talk about the future," he said. "Our future."

Hannah took his hands in hers. "I'm not having this conversation with you right now. You've been drinking and I don't want you to say something you'll regret later."

"There's nothing about you that I will ever regret."

The thing was, Tipsy Bruce knew all the right things to say. After opening the passenger door, she said, "Let's go home."

He slid into the seat and pulled the seat belt across his torso. As the latch clicked into place, she stepped back, ready to close the door. “I like that,” said Bruce. “Going home with you. It’s been a long time since I wanted that…”

His words left her lightheaded, and she needed to stop this conversation before it got started. Drawing in a deep breath, she filled her lungs to the point of pain. “I think you’re a little more than a little tipsy,” she said. “Let’s talk about all this in the morning—or whenever your headache wears off.”

Shoving the door, she tried to close it. Bruce stopped it with his foot. “I told you before. I’m not drunk. Maybe a few beers gave me some liquid courage. But we’ve been practically living together for two weeks.” He let out a huff of a breath. “Hell, there’s *no* practically about it. I have a right to know what you’re thinking.”

The wedding—as lovely as it had been—picked at a sore. It showed that people could grow and change and find love. But what about her? Was she damaged goods? That meant that even if Bruce was sincere, their relationship would fail. And it would be because of her.

“Hey,” he said, dragging her from her thoughts. His voice was softer now, some of the bite of anger was gone. “What are you thinking?”

Hannah shook her head. “Honestly, I don’t know what I want.”

Bruce’s head snapped back as if he’d just been struck. She hated herself for hurting him with her words. She tried again. “I know I like you. I know that being around you has made me happy.” She didn’t add that the past two weeks were the happiest she could remember. Being that honest felt vulnerable and raw. She wasn't sure why. She trusted Bruce to a point. Maybe, she didn't trust herself.

"Happy." The one word dripped with incredulity. "You like me."

Crap. Now she'd made things worse. Hannah's eyes burned but she refused to cry. "This isn't going the way I wanted."

Bruce snorted. "Me and you both." He let go of the door. "Maybe we should head back to your place."

Your place. The phrase echoed in her skull like the peal of a broken bell. In a matter of minutes, Bruce had gone from calling her house *home* to *your place.* It was a seismic shift; only inches moved, but her life had been shaken. She let go of the door and it swung shut with its own weight.

As she walked around to the driver's side, Hannah wondered why she sabotaged her relationships. Sure, it kept her safe. It kept her from failing at love once again. But it also meant that she would forever be alone.

Decker stood in the alley beside the grocery store. The shadows hid him as he watched people leaving the wedding reception. He wasn't sure what surprised him more—that Ryan had gotten married or that his new wife was a sheriff's deputy.

So much had changed since they'd sworn to be blood brothers. But some things had stayed the same. Decker hated to be made to look like a fool and he still loved the sight of blood.

His plan had been simple. He was going to kill everyone who had ever stood in his way. That's why he'd come back to Encantador. His first victim would be Ryan Steele—the one whose betrayal had cost Decker everything. But as he watched Bruce and Hannah quarrel, his plans changed. It seemed that the survivors from the desert had become a couple. Decker felt certain that they'd bonded over the trauma of surviving him. It seemed only fitting that they be the first to die. He walked toward his car, parked behind a dumpster. Was it the same garbage bin where he'd dumped a body years earlier, when he'd first learned that he was the descendant of Jack the Ripper? He thought it might just be. But now was no time for nostalgia.

He eased the car door open slowly, careful not to make a sound. He closed it with the same caution. Turning on the ignition, he left the lights off and rolled backward. By the time he came to the end of the block, the SUV drove by.

Through the SUV's passenger window, he could see Bruce. The man's jaw was tight, and his hard stare was trained forward. In short, he looked miserable.

Decker would let him wallow in his self-pity for now. Soon enough he would understand real suffering. Keeping his lights off while he drove, Decker hung back nearly a quarter of a mile. It was far enough away that Hannah would never see his car, especially at night and with no streetlights on the rural road.

It gave him room to think. To plan. To scheme.

It was fitting that he was back in Encantador. After all, it was here that he had discovered his connection to Jack the Ripper. This was what had inspired him to go on a killing spree and work with the hacker known as Seraphim. Decker wanted to be the most famous serial killer of all time. His mistake had been to rely on others.

It was only luck that had enabled him to stay one step ahead of the authorities as long as he had. Well, luck and his own cunning.

Ahead, the SUV's blinker flickered as it slowed to make a turn.

"What an effing do-gooder. Who the hell is on the road to see you?" he asked, though he was by himself. "Christ-a-mighty," he grumbled.

Letting his foot off the gas, he rolled to stop. From the road, he watched as the headlights cut a path through the darkness as Hannah drove to a lone house sitting atop a rise. Soon, the couple would be inside and too distracted by their fight to notice Decker. He'd killed enough people to know that their anger would make them an easy target.

He eased his car onto the road's shoulder. He turned the key, stilling the engine. Already, he could feel the flesh around Hannah's throat as he choked the life out of her. He could already see the light of her life vanish from her eyes. Then, he'd disembowel Hannah and leave her body as a warning to all.

Decker Newcombe was back.

The man, of course, would have to die first. It didn't matter that Bruce was angry and hurt now, he'd always try to be a hero. Tucking the car keys into his pocket, Decker opened the door and stepped into the night.

He started walking toward the house. This time, he

was on his own. This time, Decker would succeed. This time, he would do more than exact his revenge. He'd make sure that the world knew his name and feared him.

Chapter 19

Bruce had screwed up. He and Hannah had already discussed a permanent commitment. He knew what she wanted; she had asked that he not press for more than she was willing to give. She needed time to trust him—to trust herself—before giving her heart away another time. But dammit all, after years of living in the fog of grief, he wanted to be with Hannah. Not just now—but always.

The SUV slowed as Hannah stopped next to where his truck sat and put the gear into Park. She left one hand on the steering wheel and stared through the windshield. The interior lights bathed her in a silvery glow, turning her lips dark red and her hair to ebony. His fingers itched with the need to trace the line of her shoulder and neck. But he wasn't sure if she'd welcome his touch.

"Hannah," he said, his voice swallowed by the engine noise. Still, she must've heard him. She looked in his direction. "I don't know how things got so off track this evening," he said. "I'm sorry…"

She raised her hand, and he let his apology die on his lips.

"There's nothing for either one of us to be sorry for. You know what you want. There's nothing wrong with that. It's just..." Now it was her turn to let her words unspool. "It's just I wasn't ready for what you said tonight. About us being together forever. About this being your home." She pressed her lips together and he held his breath. Bruce silently prayed that she would give him a reason to hope. Instead, she turned off the engine. "We need to talk," she said. "But not tonight."

"Do you want me to leave?" A thick sludge of anger and hurt filled his veins. He started to sweat. Loosening his tie, he continued. "Do you want me to pack up and just go?"

"That's not what I said. But if you're going to get mad at me, then yeah, maybe you should go back to your house."

Double dammit. Why couldn't he just keep his big mouth shut? Maybe there was something to Hannah's theory about Bruce letting the beer talk for him. Everything he'd said had been true, but he couldn't stay here now. After unbuckling his seat belt, he shoved the car door open. Hopping to the ground, he stalked up the steps to the door.

Since Hannah was the only one with a key, he was forced to wait as she unlocked the front door. Gypsum waited on the threshold. The dog gave a happy bark as he stepped inside. He wasn't in the mood to be companionable and ignored the canine as he climbed the stairs to the bedroom. He could feel Gypsum's disappointment that he hadn't taken the time to greet her.

It was too late to go back now.

In the guest bedroom, he pulled his belongings out of a spare drawer and shoved them into his duffel bag.

His keys sat on top of the dresser, and he shoved them into his pants' pocket. Next, he made his way to the hallway bathroom. In a cup on the vanity, his toothbrush rested next to Hannah's in a holder. Wrapping his fingers around the handle, he stopped. He could leave a few personal items behind. Then, in a day or two, he would ask to come around and pick them up. It would give him an excuse to see Hannah again.

No. He wasn't going to play games. He grabbed the toothbrush and his razor and returned to the bedroom. His bag sat on the bed. He shoved both personal care items into the side pocket of his duffel and hefted it onto his shoulder. He walked down the steps.

Gypsum sat at the foot of the stairs, watching him with sad eyes. "Hey, girl," he said, scratching her behind the ears. "You're a good dog. You take care of Hannah for me."

She thumped her tail slowly. The sound reverberated through the floorboards with the cadence of a death march. Hannah came out of the kitchen. She'd taken off her shoes. Her toenails had been painted red. Despite his anger and hurt, he found that detail sexy. Sexier still knowing that she'd taken the time to paint her nails for him. After all, he was the only one who would see her barefoot.

An apology clung to his lips. He need only open his mouth and the words *I'm sorry* would come out. And he was sorry. Hell, they'd only known each other for a few weeks. She was wise to pump the breaks on the relationship.

But his jaw remained clenched, and Bruce remained silent.

Folding her arms across her chest, she leaned against the wall. "Looks like you have everything."

He searched her face and her tone for a hint of her emotions. There was nothing there to read. Her calm was like gasoline on a fire and left Bruce madder than before. "I made sure to get everything."

She pushed off the wall and took two steps toward him. "I'd like to talk again. Not tonight, but maybe in a few days. Can I call you?"

She was throwing him a lifeline. And what's more, Bruce felt like he was drowning. All he needed to do was reach out to her. To say he was sorry.

Just say it, damn you. Tell her that even if they needed a night apart, he'd welcome her call in the morning. He'd come back, if she still wanted him. They could start over and slow things down. Yet the words stuck in his throat.

Bruce hated himself for being so stubborn.

"Call if you want," he said, shrugging the bag higher on his shoulder.

She opened the door, letting in a gust of cool evening air. "All right, then. I guess you better..."

"All right, then," he echoed, and stepped across the threshold. He walked down the steps and stopped next to his truck. With his hand resting on the handle, he made himself a promise. If she was watching from the door, he'd go back, take Hannah in his arms and kiss her. He'd promise to take things slow, even though he was eager to start his life with her.

Bruce drew in a deep breath and glanced over his

shoulder. The door was closed. He exhaled, emptying his lungs in a single gust. His chest was hollow and hurt like hell. But he embraced the pain. It would remind him not to care for someone again.

After unlocking the latch, he opened the truck door. He tossed his bag across the console. It landed on the passenger seat and teetered before falling onto the floor. His toothbrush slipped out of the side pocket and landed on the grimy mat. *That's just the way tonight's going*, he said to himself.

He climbed into the driver's seat and pulled the door closed. Metal hit metal with a clang and he started the engine. The porch light went dark, and then the glow behind the entryway window dimmed, as well. Hannah must've been waiting for him to leave before turning off the lights.

To him, the darkness felt final.

He shifted into Reverse and backed up enough to turn around and drive down the lane leading to the county route. As gravel met blacktop, he glanced in the rearview mirror. The house was dark, except for a single window. It was Hannah's bedroom. How was he driving away instead of staying inside with her?

He pulled onto the road and headed toward his house. His headlights cut through the night, and the light reflected off metal and glass. He slowed as he came up next to a car that was parked on the road's shoulder.

From where he sat, he could see into both the front and back seats. Nobody was in the vehicle. He hadn't seen anyone walking on the road. Had the abandoned car been sitting there when they'd driven by before?

Honestly, Bruce couldn't remember. He'd been too focused on his own despair to pay attention to anything else. He looked at the vehicle again and a shiver ran down his spine.

Sure, the old car might not be anything other than a broken-down jalopy. But what if it wasn't? Over the past two weeks, nobody had seen Decker Newcombe. He hoped he was gone. Had that been wishful thinking?

The killer was still at large. Pulling the phone from his pocket, he opened his contact app and pulled up Hannah's number. He pressed the phone icon, and the call began to ring.

"Come on," he said, pleading with the night. "Pick up."

Hannah stood in the bathroom and regarded her reflection in the mirror. Water from the tap sluiced over her fingers and circled down the drain. The makeup—foundation, blush, eyeshadow and mascara that she'd taken so much time to apply—had smudged and settled into the creases and lines of her face, adding years to her appearance. But it was more than just the cosmetics that had aged her. Regret, a hard knot, sat on her gut and showed on her face.

She shouldn't have let Bruce leave. Certainly, there was something she could have said to make things right.

Despite his demeanor, she'd call him in the morning.

Tonight, she would rest, reset, and hope that there was clarity when she woke.

She pumped several squirts of cleanser onto her fingertips and began to scrub the makeup off her cheeks.

In the bedroom, her phone began to chime. She quickly rinsed off the cleanser. Patting her face dry, she walked across the hall. Gypsum lay on the mattress and looked up as she entered. The ringing ended. Hannah glanced at the phone's screen. There was a single message.

One missed call. Bruce McDaniel.

She waited for a voicemail to appear. One minute. Another. Nothing came through.

She sighed. Did she call him back? Wait for him to say something to her? Just because she wasn't ready to commit to forever didn't mean that she wanted to break up. Walking back across the hall, she finished washing her face.

With her face clean, she picked up a tube of an expensive nighttime moisturizer. It was the one indulgence in her beauty routine. As Hannah rubbed the cream into her neck and chest, Gypsum raised her head. The dog's ears perked up, and she let out a low growl.

"What is it, girl?" Massaging in the last of the moisturizer, she crossed the hallway from the bathroom to the bedroom. "Do you hear something?"

Bruce had been staying with her for only two weeks. But in that short time, she'd gotten used to his company. What's more, without him, she truly understood that she was alone and exposed.

The dog growled again. Hannah placed her hand on Gypsum's back. "Shhh," she shushed.

With the quiet, she could hear the crunch of footfalls on gravel. The tread was heavy. It was a man's step. Not just any man. It had to be Bruce. He'd come back. Her heart hammered against her chest as the warmth of hope flooded her veins. Maybe he'd accidentally left something behind. Maybe he wanted to apologize or work out their differences. Why he'd returned didn't matter. Hannah wouldn't waste another chance. She wasn't sure how, but she'd find a way to fix things with Bruce. Taking the steps, she descended to the first floor.

Outside, she could hear the hollow thump of steps on the porch. Without thought, she unlatched the lock and pulled the door open. The shadow of a man stood on her stoop. Her blood cooled.

Then the man took another step forward. A beam of light fell out of the open door and shone on his face. Without question, Decker Newcombe had found her.

Decker smiled and watched the color drain from Hannah's face. She'd made it all too easy for him by opening the door before he even had to break in.

"You," she said, her voice trembling.

"Expecting someone else?" he asked.

He knew she was hoping that Bruce had come back. But Decker had hidden at the edge of her property and watched as the other man had driven away.

She slammed the door shut and the bolt engaged with a click. Dammit. He hadn't expected her to react so quickly. He rushed forward and slammed both of his fists against the door. The frame shuddered. "Open up," he demanded. "And I'll go easy on you."

"Get off my property," she said. "I have a gun. I've shot you once before and I'll do it again."

Without thought, Decker's hand drifted to his side. The bullet wound had turned into a puckered red scar and his flesh was still tender. He'd lied when he said that he would go easy on Hannah. He was going to make her sorry that she'd ever fired a gun in his direction.

Inside the house, the dog barked and snarled. He didn't like killing animals. But he wasn't going to let himself get mauled by the damned dog. It meant he couldn't just smash a window and force his way inside. Besides, Hannah might really have a gun…

A set of headlights cut through the gloom, shining on him from behind. Even with the glare from the beams in his face, he recognized Bruce's truck. The vehicle was moving fast, and if Decker wanted to escape, he had to leave now.

Jumping over the side of the porch, he landed on his hands and knees. His legs creaked as he ran into the night. But this fight wasn't over. As far as he was concerned, it had just begun.

Bruce watched Decker run away. He was swallowed by the darkness. He wanted to give chase, but he needed to make sure that Hannah was safe first. He bounded up the porch steps, taking them two at a time. "Hannah," he said, calling through the jamb. "Are you in there? Are you hurt? Say something."

"Bruce." Her voice quavered. "Is that you? Where's Decker?"

"He ran off when he saw my truck. I don't know where he went, but he couldn't have gone far."

The lock disengaged with a click. She opened the door. "Come in," she said. "Hurry."

He crossed the threshold. She slammed the door

closed and then engaged the lock. “Holy crap,” she said, “he just showed up at my house. I heard him outside and opened the door.”

“You opened the door…” He couldn’t keep the disbelief from his tone.

She bit her bottom lip. “I thought it was you. I’d thought you come back.” She paused. “I’d hoped that you’d come back.”

So, she wasn’t through with him—with them. Not yet. But for the moment, there were more important things to worry about. “Did you call the police?”

“No. My phone’s in the bedroom.” She passed him on her way to the stairs. “I’ll go get it.”

He grabbed her arm. His palm warmed. Their gazes met. He wanted to hold her. To touch her. To kiss her and tell her it was going to be all right. But a killer was at their door, and Bruce wasn’t sure what would happen next. “I’ve got my phone,” he said, taking the device from his pocket. “I’ll make the call.”

He didn’t dial emergency services, instead, dialing the sheriff’s personal number. Mooky Parsons answered after the third ring. “Bruce? That you? It’s late. What’s going on?”

“He’s here,” he said. “At Hannah’s place. Decker Newcombe is outside.”

“Holy shit,” said the sheriff. “You sure?”

“We both saw him, Sheriff. I don’t know how he found us or what he wants…” Then again, he knew what Decker was after—they all did. He’d come to finish what he’d started. He was going to kill Hannah and Bruce—the two people who’d survived.

"I'm going to call in the Texas Rangers, the FBI and Texas Law. But I'm coming to you. If you're inside and he's outside, stay put. Help is on the way. I'll be there in a minute." Then the sheriff ended the call.

Bruce stared at the phone before turning to Hannah.

She placed her hand on his arm. "I'm glad you're here. I'm glad you came back."

The need to kiss her was too much. He placed his lips on hers. "I'll always be around when you need me."

Gypsum sat at their feet. The dog looked at the door and whined. Was Decker just outside? When Bruce was in the hospital, his shotgun had been taken by the FBI for forensic testing. He hadn't bothered to ask for it back. He saw that as a mistake now. Hannah's gun had been taken by the feds, as well. So, she didn't have any firearms in her house, either. It meant that if Decker broke in, they'd have to fight him off by hand. The notion left Bruce sick to his stomach. "Help is on the way," he said as much to himself as to Hannah. "Decker has to know that we called the police. He's a wily son of a bitch and has probably taken off already."

Hannah moved closer. Her breasts pressed against the side of his arm. "Do you smell that?"

He sniffed and recognized the scent immediately. Acrid smoke wafted through the entryway, turning the air hazy. Bruce had been wrong. Decker hadn't left. In fact, he'd set fire to Hannah's house. It was a sure way to force them into the open for a final showdown.

Chapter 20

Decker used accelerant to souse a row of bushes that lined the back of the house. He threw a match on the branches and flames sprang up immediately. It wouldn't be long before Bruce and Hannah came out of the house.

He assumed that they'd called the police. It meant that law enforcement was already on their way. But Decker refused to waste this chance. Before the cops showed up, the couple needed to be dead, and he needed to be gone. Standing in the shadows, he watched the front door and waited. It was a calculated move on his part. Sure, there was a rear door on the property. But flames licked across the entire back wall of the house. And there was another reason he assumed that they'd come out of the front door. It was the shortest distance to the vehicles that were parked on the driveway.

The seconds ticked by with the beating of his heart. He watched and waited.

"Come on," he urged. They had to smell the smoke by now. They had to be discussing what should be done and gauge the biggest threat. Over the years, Decker had learned that the fight for self-preservation was paramount. They'd leave a burning house, even if it meant coming face-to-face with a killer. Of that, he was certain.

Yet the seconds turned into minutes.

Were they calling his bluff? Did they have an ETA for law enforcement or the fire department—one that was sooner than he'd guessed? Could they really wait him out and stay inside?

The thought that he might fail burned in his gut with more intensity than the fire that charred the wood facade. From where he stood, he stared at the edge of the property and the road beyond. He looked for the telltale sign that first responders were on the way. The glow of red or blue from emergency lights. He listened for the wail of distant sirens.

There was nothing beyond the shadows of undulating flames and the crackle as the hungry fire devoured the bushes and consumed the house. He waited a minute and then a minute more. He imagined the first floor, filled with smoke that burned their eyes and clawed at their throats and lungs.

There was a sharp crack as glass broke. It was a window at the back, shattering with the heat from the fire. Or maybe they'd broken a window to escape? No, they'd never be able to climb through the flames.

He stared at the front door and willed it to open.

They had to come out. Now. Now. Now.

Another thought came to him, filling his gut with sludge.

What if they were already unconscious? What if they'd died from smoke inhalation already?

He wanted to scream and curse. He could see the

headline now: Infamous Killer Uses Arson on Latest Victims.

Then the door opened. A cloud of smoke billowed out of the sliver between door and jamb. A moment later, it opened farther. Hannah and her dog stumbled onto the porch. Hannah held a cloth over her own nose and mouth, and the dog's snout. Bruce followed.

Decker stayed in the shadows and watched. Hannah didn't carry a gun. Neither did Bruce.

All the talk about the firearm had been a ruse. The dog stumbled down the steps and retched on the grass. Coughing and wheezing, Hannah and Bruce followed. That's when Decker stepped out of the darkness. Sparks shot skyward as the roof caught fire. The scent of smoke filled the air, drying his eyes and burning his lungs. He didn't care about the discomfort.

"I wondered how long it was going to take you both to get outside. You had me worried. I thought you'd died."

Bruce stood hunched over, his hands on his knees. It would be easy to shoot him in the back of the head. But Decker had sold all his weapons just to get enough money to buy a car and fuel for the trip to Texas.

But he didn't need a gun. Both were sick from the effects of the smoke. They were weak. Killing them would be easy. With a running start, he kicked Brucc, aiming for the spot where the man had been shot only weeks before. Bruce rolled to his back and moaned, a protective hand across his chest.

Hannah screamed. "No!"

The dog barked, and lunged at Decker. He kicked at the mutt, barely missing its muzzle.

"Gypsum, come." Hannah pushed herself onto her hands and knees. Coughing, she spat on the ground. Then she wheezed, "Leave Bruce alone, you bastard."

Leaving Bruce alone was the last thing he intended to do. He kicked him again, his boot connecting with a satisfying thud. Bruce deserved to suffer. But Decker didn't have much time to make his play. He had to kill the man now.

He dove for Bruce, wrapping his hands around the man's throat. For a moment, he was filled with power. He was going to be a legend. People would talk about Decker for centuries to come—just like they did with his ancestor, Jack the Ripper. He would be the evil that lurked in the shadows long after his body turned to dust. He squeezed harder, felt the flesh compress under his palms.

Decker didn't take time to wonder why Bruce wasn't fighting back. He was never curious about why Hannah hadn't attacked him from behind. Or why the dog hadn't bitten him already. He only realized his mistake an instant before he saw the glint of metal reflecting in the firelight. Bruce held the handle of a knife. Without a word, he drove the blade between Decker's ribs.

For a moment, he felt nothing, and wondered if somehow the blade had missed. But a river of blood flowed down his chest. Hot and metallic, it stained his shirt. Decker went cold for an instant, and then the pain crashed down on him with the force of an avalanche. His arms were weak, and his hands went numb.

Bruce shimmied, sliding out from under Decker. The ground beneath Decker seemed to tilt. Falling to his back, he watched as clouds of smoke drifted across a sky filled with stars. The knife stuck out of his chest. His palms were slick with sweat and blood. He touched the hilt. In the distance, he heard an agonized cry. Then he realized that he was the one who was screaming.

In his periphery, he could see the couple. They stood to the side and held each other. He wondered if they'd recovered quickly after being in the fire—or if it had been a trick all along.

Panting, he pulled the knife free. Blood gushed out of the wound. He pressed his hand to the injury, but it was no use. His life's blood was leaking through his fingers. In the distance, he heard the wailing of sirens. Blue and red lights strobed against the darkness.

Decker's time was up.

There was the growl of an engine and the squeaking of breaks before a car door opened and slammed shut. Ryan Steele's face came into his vision. His eyebrows were drawn together and his mouth was pressed into a grim line.

Decker wanted to chuckle. "Don't tell me that you're worried about me."

"It didn't have to be this way," said Ryan.

"We both knew I wasn't going to grow old." He paused, realizing that he could no longer feel his legs. Funny to think that he'd taken so many lives and now death had finally come for him. "I'm going to Hell. I know that."

"You don't know what comes after all of this," said Ryan.

"I'm going to Hell," he said again, "and I'll save you a seat."

Then Decker was in the dark and part of the void at the same time. His chest no longer hurt. The stench of fire and ash no longer hung in the air. There was a bright light at the end of a long tunnel. He moved toward the light. It ended in a forest. He was surrounded by trees and dappled sunlight and the song of birds. There was a firepit surrounded by stones. A small tent sat on the ground. He recognized it at once. It was the wooded area that rose up around the small trailer park where he'd lived as child. It was the one place that Decker had been happy, and now he was home.

One month later

The sun had set not long before. The lone farmhouse sat on a ridge like a beacon in the desert. Bruce stood in the kitchen and scooped servings of shepherd's pie onto three plates. From the living room came the sound of female voices.

"It's about to start," said Shana. "Hurry up, Dad."

"Do you need a hand?" asked Hannah.

Bruce set all three plates on a large tray. "I've got it," he said, adding forks and napkins. "I'm coming."

After the fire, Hannah had had to move out of her house. She'd stayed with Bruce on the ranch, but they'd both known that was temporary. A local contractor had brought a crew who worked from sunup to sundown. Enough of the repairs had already been completed for her to move back to her place. Bruce had come with her.

Holding the handles of the tray, he walked down the hallway. The living room was at the front of the house and the faint scent of smoke still hung in the air. He set the tray on the coffee table. Hannah rose from her seat and picked up a plate, along with a napkin and fork. She held it out to Shana. "Here you go."

Shana sat in a recliner and leaned forward to take the plate. Settling back in the chair, she used her fork to scoop up a bite of meat, potatoes, veggies and sauce. "Mmm," she hummed. "You have become one heck of a cook, Dad. This is better than anything I could make."

Hannah handed him a plate and Bruce sat on the sofa.

"Come over sometime," he said. "I'll give you lessons."

Shana took another bite. "Let's set up a date."

A TV hung on the wall. The commercial ended and the set of a newscast filled the screen. "We're back in studio," said a male announcer, "and want to turn it over now to our crime reporter, Rita Martinez."

The camera panned to a dark-haired woman who Bruce had gotten to know well over the past month.

"There she is," said Hannah, taking the final plate from the tray and sitting down next to Bruce. She took a bite of shepherd's pie. "This is excellent," she said. "You've outdone yourself this time."

"I changed up the spices a little," he said, thinking that this meal, this night, was just about perfect. He stopped speaking and turned his attention to the TV.

On the screen, Rita said, "It was one month ago today when the infamous serial killer Decker Newcombe died during yet another attempted murder. I had the opportunity to visit with the two people who finally stopped

Decker and ended a communities' nightmare. Watch this."

The image on the screen changed again. The picture had been taken in this very room. Bruce and Hannah were on the screen and sitting in almost the same places they now sat.

"There you both are," said Shana, waving at the TV with the same excitement she had as a kid on Christmas morning. "You two look great."

Hannah playfully pushed Bruce with her shoulder. "You definitely look great."

"You look better." He nudged her back.

Since Decker's death, Bruce had done several interviews. He knew that the public was interested in the case and felt it was his duty to make sure the story told was the truth. Giving a good interview was a skill—one that he had learned by making a few mistakes along the way.

"This is going to be the last time I talk to the press, so I hope I sound great, too."

Back on the TV, Rita asked, "The last time we spoke on camera, you were being released from the hospital, Bruce. How are you feeling now? Have all your injuries healed?"

"I can tell when it rains," he said, partly joking and partly telling the truth, "because my shoulder hurts. But I've gotten back most of my range of motion. I'm back working on the ranch and putting in close to a full day."

"What about you, Hannah? How are you?"

"Everything that happened with Decker will stay with me forever. But I'm getting through each day. Keeping busy. Making friends. I see a therapist to work through the post-traumatic stress, and that helps. But mostly, I rely on Bruce." On the screen, she looked at him and smiled. Bruce smiled back. Even now, he could see the look of adoration on his face. It was obvious to the world that he was smitten. "After everything we went through together, we definitely have a strong bond."

"Is there more between you than just having survived Decker Newcombe?"

"Definitely," said Hannah.

In the interview, Bruce reached for her hand. Now, he reached for her hand in real life, too.

On TV, Bruce repeated, "Definitely."

Rita said, "Let's go back to the night that Decker showed up at your house. You had come back from a wedding and Bruce had left..."

"We'd had an argument," said Hannah. "As he was driving away, he noticed that a car was parked on the side of the road. Instead of ignoring it, he came back. It saved my life," she said, squeezing his palm.

Bruce picked up the story. "I saw Decker running off when I came up the drive. We barricaded ourselves in the house and called the sheriff. That's when Newcombe set fire to the bushes out back. Texas Law had put in a security system, so the fire department got an automatic alert that there was a blaze. They got here quick enough to save the house, even though there was some damage."

"Back to Decker," said Rita. "How did you end up killing him? So many people tried—and everyone failed—until you."

Bruce glanced at Hannah. He recalled those moments as the house filled with smoke. At the time, they'd hoped to be able to stay inside until emergency services arrived. But it had gotten hard to breathe and they'd known that they would have to leave or else they would die. They'd also known that going outside meant facing Decker and they would have to be prepared.

"Decker had bragged to us that he'd hidden a knife on his person and had stabbed Ezra—one of the Texas Law operatives—in the neck. To me, it seemed only fair to play the game using Decker's rules. I grabbed a kitchen knife and hid it in my suitcoat, and we went outside."

"It's hard to say that we hoped Decker would attack, but he did," said Hannah. "Decker was so savage—it was hard to watch. But we knew the only way to finally stop the killer was to make him think he'd won."

On the screen, they were both quiet for a moment, reliving that night. "The police, ambulance and fire truck showed up moments later. By then, it was too late for Decker."

"And, obviously, you won't be charged with any crimes personally," noted the reporter.

Hannah said, "There was an investigation. It was determined that we were acting in self-defense."

"So, what's next for you?" asked Rita.

"Well..." Hannah began. "The house is still being repaired after the fire. I'm still training dogs. We're putting in a kennel soon, so I can start to board pets. Maybe I'll offer doggie day care, as well."

"Those are all great plans professionally. What about personally?" Rita asked.

"Right now..." Bruce looked at Hannah and smiled. "We're taking it one day at a time."

The picture on the screen changed to the studio. "Take life one day at a time," Rita paraphrased. "Good advice from a brave couple."

A commercial began to play. Shana lifted the remote from the coffee table and muted the TV. "You both did amazing," she said.

Bruce agreed. "We did do amazing."

"Looks like we make a good team," said Hannah. She still held his hand.

"Well, I'm going to go before you two get overly lovey-dovey."

"You didn't finish your dinner," said Bruce.

"I'll get a leftover container and take it with me," she said, rising from her seat. "If that's okay with you, Hannah?"

"You are welcome to anything in my house," she said, standing, as well. "But I can get a dish for you."

Shana picked up her plate. "You stay put. I know where everything is—and you need to eat your dinner, too."

Bruce's daughter left. Gypsum rushed to her feet and followed. Like always, her toenails clicked on the hardwood floor.

Hannah took a bite of the shepherd's pie. She was silent for a moment, and then she asked, "Are you really okay taking things one day at a time—with us, I mean?"

"Honestly, I'm happy with where we are. And I believe that we have a future together. So, yeah. I'm fine."

She scooped up another bite onto her fork, but didn't eat. "I know that I've fallen in love too fast before. If we're together after a year, we can revisit a more permanent commitment."

Bruce did a bit of mental math. "There are fifty-two weeks in a year. We've been together for six weeks already. That means we only have forty-six more weeks left."

"It sounds like a really long time when you put it that way," she said.

"It feels like an eternity," said Bruce. "But that's okay. I want to be with you forever anyway."

He leaned toward Hannah and placed his lips on hers. He knew this kiss was just the beginning of their happily-ever-after.

* * * * *